BEGIN HERE

You are about to meet Lucas. He is French, living in France, but he could be a boy of any nationality, living anywhere. His story is universal. And it's a story that is happening every day.

This novel is about addiction to pornography. The cyber-porn issue is an uncomfortable one, and it's easy to squirm when the topic comes up. But it needs to be talked about. It is alarming to note that there is a whole segment of cyber-porn produced specifically for teenagers. And like a lot of adults, teenagers are ill-equipped to deal with the onslaught of pornographic images that hurtle at them. Paradoxically, the culture of porn has seeped into the everyday vocabulary of teens, where it has established a concept of sexuality based on the roles of the men and women in the videos. The result is that many girls begin to think that sex that runs counter to their innermost desires is normal. Likewise, boys end up with a fear of not measuring up to the performance of male porn stars.

Point of View is meant for all readers: boys, girls, parents, educators, and health professionals. It can help put difficult things into words, especially on a topic where words have been sorely missing. Please read this universal story.

Translation copyright © 2019 by Françoise Bui

All rights reserved. Published in the United States by Delacorte Press, an imprint of Random House Children's Books, a division of Penguin Random House LLC, New York. Originally published in paperback in France as *P.O.V. Point of View* by Éditions SYROS, Sejer, Paris, and edited by Natalie Beunat, in 2018. Copyright © 2018 by Éditions SYROS, Sejer.

Delacorte Press is a registered trademark and the colophon is a trademark of Penguin Random House LLC.

Visit us on the Web! GetUnderlined.com

Educators and librarians, for a variety of teaching tools, visit us at RHTeachersLibrarians.com

Library of Congress Cataloging-in-Publication Data
Names: Bard, Patrick, author. | Bui, Françoise, translator.
Title: Point of view : a novel / Patrick Bard ; translated from the French by Françoise Bui.
Other titles: POV. English
Description: First American edition. | New York : Delacorte Press, [2019] | Summary: From the first time he accidentally saw pornography online, Lucas, now sixteen, has been addicted and as he sets out on the road to recovery, he helps mend his family, as well.
Identifiers: LCCN2018056576 | ISBN 978-1-9848-5176-5 (trade hardcover) | ISBN 978-1-9848-5177-2 (ebook)
Subjects: | CYAC: Pornography—Fiction. | Compulsive behavior—Fiction. | Family problems—Fiction. | Counseling—Fiction.
Classification: LCC PZ7.1.B37057 Poi 2019 | DDC [Fic]—dc23

The text of this book is set in 11.5-point Adobe Text Pro.
Interior design by Ken Crossland

Printed in the United States of America
10 9 8 7 6 5 4 3 2 1
First American Edition

Point of View

A NOVEL BY PATRICK BARD

TRANSLATED FROM THE FRENCH
BY FRANÇOISE BUI

DELACORTE PRESS

Point of View

PROLOGUE

"Lucas, it's time!"

Lucas blinks and opens his eyes in the dim bedroom where the red power lights of his devices act like beacons.

"Okay, Mom, getting up," he mumbles back.

The alarm didn't go off. Or at least, he didn't hear it. He stretches and gropes around until his fingers find his smartphone on the nightstand. He grips it and in one quick glide of his index finger swipes the touchscreen. Nothing happens. He frowns, brings the phone closer to his face, swipes again, still with no success. This time he sits up in bed and turns his side lamp on. He doesn't remember forgetting to charge his phone, but considering his heavy-duty use of the device, a battery problem can't be ruled out. He connects the charger to the phone and again attempts to revive it. Still nothing. He tries again and again, furiously pressing the On/Off button. He wipes his damp hands on his *Serial Gamer* T-shirt, pushes back the rumpled comforter emblazoned with an enormous *DON'T WAKE ME UP!*, and hops out of bed. Without bothering to sit down at his desk, he starts nervously tapping the trackpad of his laptop. There has to be a discussion board where someone will be able to tell him how to bring his blasted phone back to life. The computer screen comes up with the Blue Screen of Death and a frownie. That's it. Lucas feels his legs go weak. It can't be . . .

This time he pulls the desk chair toward him and collapses into it, gripped by panic. A trickle of cold sweat drips down his spine. Soon he's drenched in perspiration. It can't be happening. Not this!

He pushes the Power button and the laptop shuts off. He turns it on again and gets the same result: a big frownie. His mouth dry, his hands trembling, he attempts to power-cycle a good dozen times before giving up. He never thought this would happen to him. He's heard about it, of course, but he always assumed stories about viruses were grossly exaggerated. He's been at this for years. He's encountered a few problems, some not that long ago, in fact, but he's always worked them out. Only this time . . .

He glances around his room to find a solution, but there isn't one. He buries his tousled head in his fisted hands. After a few moments, he straightens up. Without his screens, he doesn't even know what time it is. The house is nearly silent, except for the comings and goings of his mother. He hears her shout: "Hurry up, Lucas! I'm leaving! See you tonight!" The front door slams shut. His father has already left.

Shit and double shit! Tennis. Benjamin. He almost forgot. He starts to reach for his smartphone, then remembers. Oh well, he'll get it fixed. He pulls off his T-shirt in favor of an XXXL sweatshirt with the words *I Can't, I've Got Tennis* printed on the front and hops into sweatpants. He's out of breath. He feels woolly from too little sleep and nearly as empty as if his own internal hard drive has crashed.

Which isn't far from the truth.

VANISH

1

"Lucas? Are you listening to me? You'd already left when I showed up."

Lucas looks at his dinner plate. "Well, since you weren't there," he mumbles, "I came home from tennis with Benjamin."

"On his scooter?" his mother asks, annoyed. "Did you go there with him too? I've already told you that I don't want you riding on those things. I promised to pick you up. I may have been a little late, but I gave you a heads-up. Didn't you get my text?"

Lucas shrugs. "My battery died," he says.

His father lets out an irritated sigh. "Why do we bother paying for your phone plan? It's the fifth time this week that we've sent you a text, and each time you tell us that you didn't receive it. Once, because your battery died; another time because you couldn't remember where you'd put the phone. I don't believe a word of it. You're too hooked to that thing."

His father furrows his brows and realizes that it's been

a while since he's seen Lucas with his cell phone in hand. It had escaped him until now because he's just as guilty of checking Twitter at the dinner table. Like his son, he's often present without really being there.

"Say, where exactly is your smartphone?" he asks.

Lucas makes grooves on the plate of mashed potatoes getting cold in front of him. All three of them are sitting in the dining room that opens onto the living area, where a giant flat-screen TV broadcasts soundless images of some war, from somewhere in the world.

His father splatters a little sauce on the tablecloth that his mom took the trouble to spread over the Ikea table.

"Could you be more careful, Sebastian! It's going to get stained," Marie snaps at him.

"Sorry." He considers Lucas and says, "Don't tell me it was stolen again?"

"Well . . ."

This time Sebastian looks at his son closely.

"What do you mean, 'Well'? And stop thinking about how you're going to answer me. Yes or no? It's not complicated."

"It froze up. I need to reboot it."

"Now you tell us!" his mom says, rolling her eyes. "What took you so long? How have you lasted so many days without your precious phone? What an achievement!"

Lucas lowers his fork next to the cold mashed potatoes.

"Very funny, Mom," he says.

Sebastian bangs the table with his fist.

"Please don't use that tone to answer your mom. And

you're going to wipe your cell phone right after dinner. I'm not paying your bill for nothing."

"Come on, Dad. It's not the end of the world. I think the phone's dead. Might as well buy a new phone, or a tablet, since I don't have one."

"Let's try resetting it, right now," Sebastian says, getting up from the table and nodding toward the stairs that lead to Lucas's bedroom. "I'm really fed up with your lousy attitude."

"Can't we finish eating?" Marie protests in vain.

Lucas thinks he's got caricatures of adults in front of him.

It's too late. The scene degenerates into a confrontation between an alpha male and a young wolf.

"Let's go!" his father commands.

Annoyed, Lucas pushes his plate away. He follows his father, dragging his feet like a condemned man shuffling to the guillotine. Cuddles, the three-legged cat, limps after them. He purrs as he rubs himself against Lucas's shins. Lucas's look of guilt doesn't escape his dad.

"You're hiding something from me," Sebastian says as he opens the door of his son's room.

Aside from the general disarray, the sour-smelling room in no way resembles that of a typical teenager. There's nothing at all on the walls. The wooden beams are painted white, just as Lucas wanted them. There's merely an unmade bed, all topsy-turvy. Dirty socks strewn on the floor. Bunched-up clothes. Mismatched sneakers tossed every which way. Cuddles's cat bed, which he scorns in favor of Lucas's jumbled comforter, and onto which he hops with surprising agility for a maimed animal. His spotlessly clean litter box.

A printer rests on the floor, along with a dresser, its open drawers overflowing with T-shirts and pants. There isn't even enough tech equipment for it to be the bedroom of a geek. Only a lamp and school stuff and three empty bottles of Coke.

"It stinks in here," his dad says, frowning. "Don't you ever open the windows?"

He turns to Lucas and tousles the greasy hair plastered to his son's head. Lucas immediately steps back.

"And do you shower from time to time?" his dad asks. "You actually stink. Just because you spend hours in front of your laptop doesn't mean that you don't sweat."

His eyes suddenly rest on the table where the laptop lies dark, not even in screensaver mode.

"Are you suddenly worried about the environment? Since when do you shut off your computer?"

His father doesn't like wasting electricity. It's a matter of conviction. He's ecology-minded and hates it when computers stay continually powered up.

Without waiting for Lucas's response, he adds: "Okay, let's turn it back on."

Since his son doesn't move, he steps purposefully toward the computer. The motion snaps Lucas out of his lethargy.

"Wait, Dad. It crashed too," he says.

Sebastian freezes. "It's like a plague. What exactly have you been doing?"

"Nothing. I don't know. It must have gotten a virus."

"Did you download movies on a streaming site recently?"

"Well . . . maybe. I don't remember."

The half confession gets a hint of a smile out of Sebastian. He puts a hand on his son's shoulder. Lucas shakes it off in annoyance.

"It's not a big deal, Lucas. It happens to all of us. Even me. But you should be careful. You know what? Tomorrow, I'll take your computer and smartphone to work. Jerome will fix whatever needs fixing and he'll install a hacker-proof firewall. We should have done that long ago."

Sebastian goes to take the computer but Lucas blocks his way.

"It's not necessary, Dad. I can take care of it myself."

"So why haven't you done that, then? You spend your nights in front of your computer, your days on your cell phone, and suddenly you're not interested? What's the problem?"

"I already asked a friend. He's really glad to help me. He'll be disappointed if—"

"That's enough. I don't work at a computer firm for nothing. Even if I'm only in sales, I'm not an idiot. For both your smartphone and computer to have crashed at the same time means there's got to be a big bug. There are competent people at work who can deal with this. Jerome, for one, and he'll be happy to help. End of discussion." He goes around Lucas to grab hold of the laptop. "And give me your phone too."

2

Sebastian is feeling rather pleased. He just wrapped up a lucrative tech-equipment deal with a subsidiary of a major perfume company. The economic growth took off right after some cosmetics firms established offices in Chartres, so much so that the city is now known as Cosmetics Valley. The nickname changed the image of the town. Thanks to the booming economy, his wife found a job. Marie works in the accounting department of a perfume company located on the other side of town. They had to buy a second car, but their two incomes allow them enough to also pay the mortgage on the house, which they bought two years ago. Sebastian still remembers the exact wording of the real estate ad:

> Not to be missed! A steal at 190,000 euros, in the Eure Valley. Near schools, all main shopping, and train station—a charming two-story house, including living room, dining room,

fully equipped kitchen with eat-in area, three bedrooms, bathroom, loft office. Fenced-in garden with shed and carport. On roughly a quarter acre.

He quotes the ad whenever he tells someone about the first time they toured the house. He and his wife fell in love with it on the spot. Even his son was enthusiastic. The tennis club was nearby and he enrolled straight off, with lots of encouragement from his mother. The house is nothing like the noisy and cramped apartment where Lucas grew up in the Paris suburbs. They moved in during the dead of winter, under a snowfall. Sebastian popped open a bottle of champagne and he and Marie drank the bubbly surrounded by cardboard boxes. Sebastian is lost in the memory of it all when the phone on his desk rings. He startles and answers it quickly.

"Hello, Sebastian Delveau. How may I help you?"

"Seb? It's Jerome."

"Jerome! Great, have you fixed Lucas's devices?"

"Uh, you need to come by. . . ."

"What is it?"

"Nothing I can tell you over the phone."

3

Jerome's tone alarms Sebastian. He observes the other sales reps through the clear dividers of the open space. Most of his colleagues are absorbed in conversations with clients or suppliers. He gets up. As he arrives at the elevators, he hits the Down button, gets on, presses two, and wonders what Jerome has discovered. Jerome Loison isn't just a colleague. Twenty years earlier, the two men graduated from the same high school. Afterward, Sebastian left for the big city. Paris. That's where he and Marie met, during their first year of college. They've been together ever since. He was supportive of Marie's mental health crises. It required several stays for her at a psychiatric hospital. Diagnosis: depression. When Marie was gone for many weeks after Lucas's birth, he did his best. She relapsed when Lucas was in elementary school. This time she had to remain in the hospital for an even longer stretch. The doctor explained to Sebastian that depression is a chronic illness. Marie was put on antidepressants. It took a while to find the best prescription for her. At times she suffered from uncontrollable crying fits in the morning, seldom getting out of bed before noon. Sebastian had to manage his wife's illness, his son's education, and his job—and juggling all three had not been easy for him. He didn't have parents or family to turn to for help.

He can't foresee now that he'll one day need to explain to an investigative judge that when Lucas was in the grips of the measles epidemic that hit his elementary school and he woke up with an extremely high fever, Marie was incapable of getting out of bed to care for him. Sebastian got home from work and found his son shivering beneath his bedcovers, teeth chattering, forehead beaded with sweat. Marie slept soundly, passed out from the sleeping pills she was taking. Sebastian called for an ambulance and it ended well, but at the emergency room he'd been told that Lucas could have suffered serious consequences. After that, Marie spent three months in the hospital. Sebastian was so exhausted that he nearly asked for a divorce. But Marie's mental health improved. They overcame the crisis and celebrated their fortieth birthdays last year.

Sebastian gets off the elevator and heads down a hallway overrun with a jumble of cords, disemboweled towers, and scattered hard drives. In spite of the cooling fans in Jerome's office, or maybe because of them, the temperature is stiflingly hot. Dressed in a blue T-shirt printed with the words *I am not a geek, I'm a level 9 warlord,* Jerome is focused on a screen that partially conceals him. Sebastian only sees him from the back. In the glow of the fluorescent lights, Sebastian can't read his face.

"Come. Look," Jerome says flatly.

Sebastian goes around the desk and stands behind him. From here, he has an unobstructed view of a full-screen photo of Lucas taken two or three years before. Quickly, he calculates that his son was likely no older than fourteen. Lucas stands in his bedroom of the apartment where the family used to live in Bagneux, looking straight out, fully naked. His gaze is focused. His skin is slicked in oil from head to toe. He has an erection. Sebastian swallows. It takes him a moment before he can choke out a response.

"Damn it! He must be the victim of a pedophile."

4

At sixteen, Lucas has never kissed a girl, let alone had sex. But he's seen tens of thousands of people of all colors and backgrounds having sex in every possible position and every possible pairing. A man with a woman, a woman with a woman, a man with a man, men (one, two, three . . .) with a woman, women (one, two, three . . .) with a man, groups of men, women with women, in every possible attire, from the simplest outfit to costumes of nurses, secretaries, college students, professors, buff athletes, cheerleaders, maids—just to cite the more common ones—not to mention all types of lingerie. Lucas has seen as many getups for the men, including bodybuilder, pizza delivery guy, plumber, gardener, personal trainer, and taxi driver, all of them having sex with partners of all ages.

Lucas saw his first porn flick when he was eleven. He was with friends, at his best friend Jeremy's house. It was when Lucas's family lived in Bagneux. The boys were all gathered one weekday afternoon when they stumbled on a porn site.

Lucas watched, embarrassed, a little disgusted, but also slightly excited and, most of all, intrigued, troubled, and fascinated. Like the other boys, he pretended to be bored, as if he'd seen it all before. The video showed a woman around his mother's age and a twenty-something guy having basic sex.

"The cougars are the hot ones," Jeremy said. "They love doing it, and they know how to do it. They're experienced, and they go for young guys even like us."

Lucas shrugged, but that evening he had a lot of trouble falling asleep.

That was it? That was what sex was all about? Skin, skin, and more skin, moans, sighs. Nothing else? If that summed it up, he didn't get why everyone the world over made such a fuss about it. He was soon hit with the thought that he had been conceived that way, then pushed the vision into the recesses of his brain from which it should never have emerged. Instead, he asked himself how it would be when he had sex for the first time. How it would be when he was with a girl. And then, since he was far more interested in the Wolverine Epic Collection, he didn't really think about it anymore. But although relegated to a corner of his mind, the memory of the video never faded. It came back to him regularly. In truth, the memory returned more and more often according to the changes in his body, subtle changes at first, then increasingly visible ones.

When he started sixth grade his parents bought him a cell phone; then, at Christmas, he got a computer. His very own laptop. The idea of going on porn sites didn't cross his mind right away. He was too preoccupied visiting the pages devoted to superhero comics, a passion from his childhood. For some kids it was dinosaurs; for him it was Marvel. He went on online game sites. That was all. Then, in seventh grade, he started downloading movies and streaming pirated animated features that were just digital dumpsters of viruses, links to phishing scams and pop-ups that opened more pop-ups. Frequently, he had the impression of being caught in a spider's web from which he couldn't escape. The time he downloaded *Spider-Man* was when windows offering porn videos came up. He hit the green button, thinking he was activating the movie, but instead a page opened on a lottery that offered the chance to win an iPhone 7 if he played a game. Since he wasn't on a Mac, and because he already had a cell phone, he clicked on the X meant to close the window. He just wanted to see *Spider-Man*. Instead of the movie, another window opened, offering video games for cell phones at a cost of 2.49 euros per week. Still uninterested, he continued to hit X until he was offered the chance to meet "cougars" ready to satisfy his every fantasy. The nude photos of women caught his attention and he lingered on the large breasts and the open mouths. Right next to the photos, an animated GIF of a couple having sex popped up in a window.

His mouth dry, uncertain of his destination, he clicked on it simply because he liked the girl's face.

Two years had passed since fifth grade. He had grown quite a lot. His voice had deepened. As he watched the video that today he would dismiss as totally mundane, he experienced his first erection without quite understanding what was happening to him. The sex was filmed from the point of view of the guy as he looked at the girl. What particularly aroused Lucas was that the girl was looking straight into his eyes. At least, that was the impression he had. He didn't know yet that these types of videos are called POV, point of view, to designate a subjective camera angle. He also didn't understand that the guy was having sex while framing the scene and holding the camera. Two jobs done by one person reduced costs and maximized benefits. But Lucas was as unaware of this as he was of why the image he was seeing was so real.

Like a sponge, he was content just absorbing what he saw. Of course, he tried to recapture the initial thrill of excitement in the hours, days, and, even more so, the nights that followed. In fact, on the first of these nights, he barely slept, just kept going from one video to the next. It was easy to do, because whenever he clicked on a tiny image, one out of two times, instead of a video, a new window would open up offering a mosaic of new faces and bodies in a never-ending supply. That was how he ended up with dozens of open windows on his screen.

When his alarm went off in the morning, he jumped out of his chair. Like a spelunker climbing out of a cave, he gazed upon the dawn light as it entered his bedroom and realized that he had spent a sleepless night. In haste, he closed all the windows on the screen and put the computer to sleep. In English class that morning, he started to look at the girls in a different way; he started to visualize them in the roles in the videos he had seen during the night. He also ended up drifting off to sleep in the middle of class.

5

Lucas started all over again opening windows the following night. And the next one. And the one after. He started masturbating. He'd do it up to five times in a row. He ended up hurting. He didn't dare say anything to his father, much less to his mother. As for his friends, not a chance. He continued to watch pornos. His video habit increased. Now he couldn't go without a daily fix of porn.

This went on for several months, and his nights started to spill over onto the days. As soon as he could, he turned on "fuck 'n' sucks," as other boys called them, on his laptop and smartphone. Lucas wouldn't have used that term.

At the beginning, he watched each video through to the end. The videos lasted anywhere between three and twenty-five minutes. He quickly grew bored by the repetitive nature of sex. He started to fast-forward, skipping from the stripping to the blowjob, watching at high speed the one, two, three positions—doggy-style, riding, missionary. He barely understood what little was being said. He'd always been lousy in his English-language class at school. But his intuition kicked in and he quickly caught on. He was unstoppable. The only problem was that his vocabulary centered on a single and specific field of activity. But every day he explored a little more, broadening his knowledge. He discovered that the contents covered each aspect of everyday life, classified alphabetically on the sites: A for Adoration, Aerobic, Amputee, all the way through Y for Yacht, Yoga, and, of course, all the positions that go with each letter.

6

As a result of Lucas's sleepless nights, his grades quickly took a nosedive. He had never been an outstanding student, but as soon as he dropped below the average, his mother and father were called to a parent-teacher conference at school.

"Lucas isn't misbehaving in class," Mr. Lambert, his main teacher, explained as he spoke to his mother. "He's simply not mentally present, and he often drifts off to sleep."

With eyes lowered, hands on her lap, Marie seemed apathetic. Mr. Lambert couldn't help thinking that Lucas was a lot like her. Detached. As proof, it was Sebastian who responded, coming to his son's defense.

"All teenagers are like that, aren't they?" he said.

"It's best not to generalize, Mr. Delveau. Teenagers are exactly like adults. Each one has their own personality. The stereotype of a teenager is precisely that, a stereotype. The staff thinks that Lucas isn't adapting well to the demands of school. He'll be starting eighth grade soon. It's best to get him help before he starts to fail," Mr. Lambert replied, looking pointedly at Marie.

Since she still didn't react, he followed up with a question.

"What is Lucas's nightly bedtime?" he asked.

"What are you saying? We make sure Lucas goes to bed every night around ten, at the latest," Sebastian answered indignantly.

"Well, maybe that's not enough sleep for him. Young people his age need a lot of shut-eye, and all of them are lacking sleep. The reasons are usually too much television and too much computer time."

"I thought it wasn't good to generalize," Sebastian retorted caustically.

Mr. Lambert didn't argue. He merely suggested that Lucas get some tutoring. Sebastian agreed. But the private lessons didn't yield great results. It took a lot of effort for Lucas to reach passing grades in the last semester, barely enough to squeak into eighth grade.

7

Before long, looking at the videos on fast forward wasn't fast enough for Lucas. He started to click away furiously, in search of the next girl, the next thrill, in search of the one who would hold his attention. Sometimes he found her. It depended on a particular face, expression, pout, and body. He would then watch every porno the girl had appeared in. He would never have said *acted* instead of *appeared* to describe what he was seeing. Even though he knew that this theater of the flesh was nothing more than a big act. And when he ferreted out *the* rare pearl, he played and replayed the video dozens of times, finding nearly the same intensity of arousal as when he first masturbated in front of his screen. *Nearly* is precisely the problem. He quickly discovered that images get old. That their power dulls after repeated viewing. Seeing them again and again drains the screen of any excitement. He trained himself to turn away from whichever girls were his current obsession and resumed hunting on the web until his porn-filled brain almost forgot the X-rated stars he was obsessed with—Natacha, Katia, whatever other names the actresses went by. After days of fruitless pursuit, he returned to his objects of desire, as if rediscovering Natacha or Katia, along with his intense reactions—all the while inventing stories and creating scenarios. The difficulty was that each time, the effect dwindled a little more, until the element of surprise faded completely. Boredom set in. So he resumed his quest, browsing myriad faces of women upon myriad faces of women, clicking, looking for a few minutes, sometimes mere seconds, just long enough to get a sense before moving on to the next film. Hours went by without him being able to watch a single video all the way through. Hours that he robbed from his daily life. From his nights, his afternoons spent with friends who little by little grew detached, as he became equally indifferent to their company.

Aside from his secret life, he seemed to lead a normal teenage existence. It would require being inside his head to discover the variety of pornographic images that jostled each other in order to grasp the extent of the fantasies he'd developed about girls in his class, even about women he sees when he's riding the bus. In rare moments of clarity, Lucas wondered if he hadn't become one of those sex-obsessed crazies that the media talks about, and the thought depressed him. To reassure himself, and as a way of fleeing the world, he took refuge in his precious laptop, his precious smartphone, and his precious porn sites. He clicked at random, and the need to spice up his nights led further and further into practices he never imagined existed. Like the time he selected *bukkake* without the slightest idea what it meant—only to see actresses getting squirted with a deluge of sperm. Gross! It disgusted him. To erase those images from his mind, he hurried back to his favorite categories. Recently, he's discovered the world of cosplay—another thing he was completely ignorant about. When he saw the name *Wonder Woman* appear on the drop-down menu, his passion for superheroes immediately superimposed itself onto the porn images.

Just imagining what he could do with Wonder Woman's costume got him aroused. Right away, he hit the icon. The mere second it took for the clip to download seemed interminable. His patience was rewarded when the superhero appeared in an immaculate white kitchen where a plumber proceeded to shave her head before making her his sex slave. That cosplay story stirred him up for weeks. He found lots of other versions of Wonder Woman, as well as Catwoman, even of Batman. He also consumed lots of pornos with vampires, zombies, succubi, androids, and sexy models in Halloween costumes having sex in wild settings, in every position. He loved the role-playing videos that looked as if they'd stepped out of comic books made expressly for his generation.

Every late afternoon now, he waits impatiently for the moment when he's alone. The worst is when a thunderstorm prevents him from connecting to the internet. Because if he tried, it would fry the router.

Just like the time bolts of lightning shattered the sky in Bagneux. The firehouses were swamped with calls to deal with flooded basements. He had been in school, and no one had been home to disconnect the router.

The lightning ran in on the line and fried it. That evening there was no way to connect. To make things worse, lightning hit the cell tower that served the neighborhood and knocked it out. He couldn't even use his smartphone.

"Couldn't you have disconnected it this morning?" he grumbled to his mother.

His mother looked at him pensively. "I don't check the forecast every day upon waking," she said. "The thunderstorm came on suddenly. Your father will pick up a new box tomorrow. It's not like it's the end of the world. Surely you can live one day without the internet."

Lucas shrugged.

That evening, he joined his parents for dinner. Without thinking, he started fidgeting, continually bouncing his left knee, which made the table shake.

"Stop it, Lucas," his father told him, clearly irritated.

Lucas's leg stopped. But a minute later, the jerking started up again. His father struck the table with the flat of his hand. The dishes and silverware rattled.

"Enough, Lucas! Stop it! You're a bundle of nerves."

"What are you saying?"

"Don't take that tone with me. Since the box is fried, why don't you use the time to study your math."

Lucas raised his eyes and stared directly at his father. "Not in your dreams," he replied.

This time his father stood up. He raised his arm and pointed in the direction of the stairs.

"That's it!" he said angrily. "Go to your room!"

Lucas got up, but instead of heading toward his lair like he usually did when things weren't going his way, he grabbed his plate full of chicken and smashed it to the ground. The dish shattered and sauce spilled all over the white tiles.

"Pick that up right now!" his father yelled.

But Lucas had already stormed off and slammed his bedroom door shut. He stood still long enough to hear his parents talking.

"What in the world has gotten into him?" Marie asked.

"Probably just hormones. It's that age," his father answered.

With his stomach knotted up, Lucas gazed at his useless laptop screen.

8

By age thirteen, the mere sight of a computer keyboard gave Lucas an erection.

At fourteen, he started thinking about having sex. He wasn't going to take a girl on a date. He didn't think of it in those terms. He had no idea how to approach anyone of the opposite sex, but the idea made him think of Samira, a girl who had caught his eye. Her beautiful, thick dark hair came down her back, and her smoky eyes were underlined with kohl. For the first time in years, he had things other than the videos on his brain. He started to fantasize about kissing her. Of holding her in his arms. But what was he supposed to do? What was the next step? Did she French-kiss? Little by little, Samira invaded his thoughts. And strangely enough, not just with sexual fantasies. He found himself noticing and being surprisingly touched by how she bit her nails in class. By her low-pitched laugh. Yes, he really liked seeing her laughing.

In the pornos the guy approaches the girl, kisses her,

and then she slowly unzips his fly. The girl is always willing. Lucas assumed it would be the same with Samira.

But he wondered if he would be up to the challenge, like in the movies. If not, wasn't Samira going to laugh in his face? He just had to show her. He went to the bathroom, where he closed and locked the door and proceeded to carefully shave his body like the men in some of the videos. He grabbed a bottle of his mother's massage oil and coated himself with it, from head to toe. He contemplated the result in the mirror. He didn't think he looked bad, especially when he puffed out his already pudgy chest. As he thought about Samira and what she would do to him, he propped up his smartphone on the sink and took a selfie. A naked selfie, with an erection, all the while wondering if his manhood was the right size. His only worry was that Samira would find his penis too small. He knew porn actors were better endowed than he was, but he hoped to come close.

In between classes the next day, he gave Samira his cell phone number. He had missed a day of school the previous week and pretended that he wanted to catch up on math, which she was good at. He asked if she could text him photos of her corrected homework. She seemed surprised and hesitated, but she texted him a photo of her work during their next class.

That evening Lucas sent her his naked selfie. There was no doubt in his mind that the following day Samira would come to him, ready and willing. He was startled when he spotted her at the entrance of the school and she glared at him and said, "You have one twisted mind!" She launched into him. "What was that? Are you some sort of monster? A pervert?"

He was startled when she turned her back to him. Even more when he heard her telling her friend Melanie, "Did you see that creep?" and Melanie burst out laughing. When the group of girls who always orbited around Samira started gossiping whenever they crossed his path, and when they shot him side-eyes and laughed as they elbowed each other, Lucas knew that Samira had shared his selfie with them and that they were making fun of him.

He was deeply hurt. He was also afraid that the girls would post the photo on social media. He cursed himself out a thousand times for being careless. Samira and the girls were too embarrassed to do that. But each time they caught sight of him, it provoked fits of laughter. By the end of the year, his parents found the new house in Chartres and the family moved away during the winter school break. The incident with Samira receded into a bad memory and Lucas's wounded pride started to heal. But no one was going to get the best of him again. He was never going to try to pick up another girl. If there was any way for him to avoid talking to girls, he would do it. At least when he was in front of his screen, he controlled the situation.

9

Sebastian is disgusted and feels like someone is choking him so he can hardly breathe.

"What is it? A thing for pedophiles?" he asks when he speaks again. "Tell me, Jerome!"

Jerome pushes back his chair on wheels and turns it a half circle to face Sebastian.

"No, nothing like that. Nothing to do with pedophiles," he says. "Your kid has problems. Serious problems. His laptop and cell phone were infested with viruses and all sorts of filthy junk."

"But . . . what about that?" Sebastian says, pointing to the nude photo of Lucas.

"That? If you want my opinion, it's related to this," Jerome replies as he pulls up a whole series of pornographic photos. "Your son spends his days, even more so his nights, looking at pornos. It dates as far back as I can go inside this damned machine. Up until the crash he carefully erased his browsing history, but it just takes a thorough look through

34

the logs to find some disturbing things. Look! Twenty-four hours before his system crashed, he was changing sites every three minutes. Sometimes he stayed a little longer, but no more than five minutes, tops. From ten o'clock at night, which I guess is when he goes to his room after dinner, till five o'clock the next morning, he watched one hundred and forty porn videos. One hundred and forty."

10

Sebastian does not respond.

Stunned, he replays the conversation that he and Marie had with friends over dinner the week before. The three couples were approximately the same age, all with teen-agers at home. Lana, who works with Marie, brought up the topic. Two days prior, she had surprised her son in front of an X-rated film that he was watching on the internet.

"I'm sure our kid looks at them too," Julien, the husband of the third couple, said.

Marie immediately contradicted him. "Come on, that's an unfounded accusation. I'm sure Lucas isn't like that. I have total confidence in him. Besides, he's a loner. Boys do that together."

"What do you think, Seb?" Lana asked. "Are you as sure as Marie?"

Sebastian shrugged. "I don't think Lucas could care less

about that. He used to be into superheroes. Now, I don't know. He likes tennis. And Marie's right, he doesn't have a lot of friends. Likes to be by himself. I just don't see him watching a porn flick with friends."

How could he have been so wrong about his son?

11

Jerome quickly scrolls down Lucas's browsing history, unleashing a tsunami of unfamiliar acronyms at Sebastian: MILF, BBW, BBC, not to mention obscure terms: *bukkake,* tribbing, cosplay.

"MILF?" he mutters, going to back to the first acronym.

"Come on, Sebastian, are you for real? *Mom I'd Like to Fuck.* Otherwise known as a cougar. Don't tell me you've never watched a porno since the one we saw all those years ago?"

"Jerome, we were fourteen!"

"Well, how old is your son?"

"Okay, but we didn't spend our nights at it."

Sebastian still remembers when the two of them were in the living room at Jerome's house, watching their first VHS cassette, all the while looking feverishly over their shoulders and scared to death of being surprised by someone. The mere recollection of the acronym *VHS* sends him back in time and makes him conscious of his age. Wasn't what he did pretty much the same thing? Even if after the initial thrill, he grew bored by all the close-ups, by the rote nature of the sex, and even if his early flirting with girls quickly made him forget the artificial images of sex that he finds of no great interest today, he was nonetheless exposed to pornographic images as a teenager too. In seconds, his mind wanders. Did Marie watch porn cassettes with girlfriends when she was a teen? He's never asked her. How can Lucas sacrifice his days and nights, his education and his social life? Suddenly, Sebastian remembers something.

"Did you say 'as far back as you could go'?" he asks Jerome. "We gave Lucas the laptop for Christmas when he was in sixth grade. Did you go back that far?"

"That far is difficult. What I can tell you is that it's been going on a long time. Several years, for sure."

Sebastian ponders how old Lucas would have been. Twelve? Thirteen?

"I took a quick look, Seb," Jerome adds. "There's stuff I've never tried, not with Lucie, not with anyone. Stuff I didn't even know could be done. Violent things too. The good news is that the violent stuff isn't the majority. The bad news is that that's what's most recent. It's not nothing, Seb. Your kid has a problem. Like I said, a serious problem."

12

Lucas found the cat, or rather kitten, just before the move, on his way home from school. A panicked ball of black fur with a bloody right front leg that was twisted at an odd angle. A car must have hit it. The creature was meowing desperately, as if calling for help. Lucas crawled under a car. He managed to get hold of the animal without hurting it. As gently as he could, he snuggled the kitten in his parka and took it home.

"I told you: no animals in the house!" his mother yelled.

"He's been asking for a pet for years," his dad said, trying to moderate.

"I'll take care of it. I promise!" Lucas swore.

"Right, with any luck you'll take care of it for the first three weeks," his mother replied. "Then it'll be all on me."

Still, she gave in. They took the kitten to the vet, where its injured leg had to be amputated. And since the creature stuck like glue to Lucas, he named it Cuddles. The cat managed quite well on three legs and quickly got the hang of the house in Lèves. He grew into a handsome two-year-old tomcat. Contrary to his mom's predictions, Lucas took dutiful care of his cat—feeding him, regularly changing his litter box, brushing his fur—which Cuddles loves—and faithfully administering the various antiflea products.

In fact, Cuddles is Lucas's closest living companion. All that Cuddles requires is being stroked and being fed. Their relationship is clear and simple. Totally pure.

For Lucas, the move to Lèves corresponded with an even deeper period of solitude. He started at his new school without a past, without friends, which suited him just fine. The other students pegged him for a moody introvert. After a group of boys tried to befriend him at the tennis club where his mother forced him to register, he hardly was friendly to them, so they left him alone. He suffered taunts about his weight, but that was all. He was spending so much time in front of his computer that he was packing on more pounds than normal for his age. He wasn't just looking at videos; he was also stuffing himself with popcorn and ice cream, and despite his mom's objections, he was drinking two large bottles of Coke every day. As a result, he missed balls and got out of breath on the tennis court. It didn't take long for the group of boys to start calling him Fatso.

The porn he was watching provided comfort. It was like a refuge, something he knew by heart. The images allowed him to escape from the real world, from his mediocre grades at school, from his physical appearance, and, finally, from his life. Recently, he's discovered some new videos that disturbed him. The women get slapped during sex. He can't tell if they enjoy it, if they're really suffering, if it's a little of both, or if it's all one big masquerade. After constantly watching these films, they start to look the same, and he begins feeling a sense of monotony and frustration. At times, even after hours of viewing, he quits the screen without achieving any flicker of emotion. Not to mention achieving the same level of initial arousal. He realized that lately he was looking for some semblance of authenticity in a universe where everything is fake. For a simple, insignificant gesture that would reveal the truth of the moment—an actor who takes out his shirttail and reveals the scene of the action to the camera, or an actress who holds her hair back with one hand for the same reason, or who bothers to tie her hair away from her face before the camera starts to roll so that everything is visible. He notices these things now, latches on to them as proof of real life bursting in.

It's no wonder his computer is infested with viruses, his mailbox inundated with spam for "enlarging your penis," with hordes of imaginary girls who want to become his friends on Facebook. Until now, though, the firewall on his PC held up despite the regular appearance of pop-ups. Some of the pop-ups are totally funny, like the time when he was viewing a threesome and a window opened of a portrait of the president of France, along with a pseudo-official warning: *You are in violation of the law—you have connected to an illegal pornographic site.* He was instructed to click on the president's portrait, which would let him off with a warning and a fine. If he didn't do as told, a summons would be

42

mailed to his home. He had looked at the president, whose chest was covered with a tricolor scarf and whose legs were moving wildly on the screen. Lucas had burst out laughing. Who could possibly fall for that? He had surfed dozens of sites, and none had bothered to inquire whether he was legal. What a load of crap!

But at present, both his smartphone and laptop have crashed for good. He knows that his devices are totally infected and won't function again without the help of a specialist. Even then, he'll probably lose all his files. But that isn't the worst. The worst is that his depravity will inevitably be revealed to his parents.

It can't happen. He'd rather die. Or vanish forever. But his father took his devices to work. The cherry on top of the cake is that he'll be the laughingstock of his dad's colleagues. Everything he miraculously escaped two years ago with Samira rushes back to him. It's at that precise instant that he remembers the selfie. Suddenly, he can't remember for sure whether he tossed it in the trash, whether he cleared it out. If his father finds it, Lucas will die of shame.

Or maybe he'll flee with Cuddles under his arm. To where? He doesn't have a clue.

It's been more than a week now that he hasn't gone online and, in truth, he doesn't know what to do with himself. His hormones are raging, but that isn't the worst. He knows how to take care of himself. Worst of all is the free time on his hands, and he doesn't know what to do with it. Simply eating, petting Cuddles, and playing tennis and missing balls because he's completely out of breath do not fill the hours—hours that until now marched on without him noticing. Now the days are endless. The nights too long, especially as he wakes well before dawn and ponders how to get out of this dead end. He misses the videos. He tries to plunge back into old issues of his Marvel comics but with little success. Reading? Not his thing either.

Maybe no one will be able to restart his computer. Or his phone.

Maybe his father will offer to buy him new ones. He'll sound off about it, of course, and Lucas will promise to be careful. And he won't be lying. He'll definitely be careful next time around. He'll be a lot more cautious. He'll look twice before going on certain shady sites. He'll stick to mainstream sex. Mom-and-pop stuff. Promise. Even if a little voice deep within him murmurs that none of his promises will be kept.

The worst outcome is never a given. That's what he wants to cling to. It could be that his father will come home from work railing about the unreliability of computers and that in a few days everything will go back to the way it was before. Maybe his hard drive is fried. If that's the case, then there's no problem. He'll see. As if he could do otherwise.

13

When Sebastian tells Marie why Lucas's devices aren't working, her legs give way beneath her.

"Are you sure?"

Sebastian nods.

"How are we going to confront him about it?"

Sebastian doesn't answer right away.

He did not want to wait until the evening to tell Marie about Jerome's discovery. Was not able to wait is more like it. He called her at work and asked that she take the rest of the afternoon off. Pretending she had a raging migraine, she left the office and met Sebastian at a café near the Chartres train station.

The immediate problem is knowing what approach to take.

"There's no doubt. I'm sure of it," Sebastian confirms. "We can't act like nothing's happened."

"I know that," Marie responds as she halfheartedly stirs her coffee. Because of the antidepressants that she has never really stopped taking, she rarely drinks alcohol. "But how are we going to tell him that we know?" she asks, almost as if talking to herself.

Sebastian bites the inside of his lower lip, deep in thought.

"In my opinion," he finally answers, "he can't doubt but that we already know. As soon as I give him back his computer, all cleaned up, he'll know for sure."

"You're right; we can't just stay silent. And that nude selfie. What was it for?"

"I don't want to know, Marie. All we do know is that he didn't email it to an adult. More likely to a girl in his class at the time. We're lucky the parents didn't file a complaint. But it didn't have anything to do with pedophilia."

"Do you think we should seek out professional help? With Lucas?"

Sebastian shrugs. "He's a teenager. He's trying to find himself. He spends too much time on the internet looking at porn videos, but that doesn't make him a mental case."

"Are you trying to make less of this, Seb? There's the selfie. I'm worried about how he views women. Do you really think it's not necessary? I think it would be good for us to take him to see someone. After all, every kid his age doesn't spend all their free time on porn. And that's on top of his binge eating."

"I don't think it warrants seeing a shrink," Sebastian tells Marie. "He's getting fat because he's in front of his computer day and night."

"Still . . . ," Marie mutters, looking stubborn.

It's a look Sebastian knows well. He reaches a hand out to reassure her.

"I'll tell you what we're going to do. No more laptop. No more smartphone. No more internet. If he needs to research something for school, he'll use our computer, under our supervision. Period. He'll be forced to find something else to do, no?"

Marie pulls her hand away from Sebastian's. The creases on her forehead deepen.

"It's not enough," she says. "I'm willing to put off taking him to see a shrink, but we have to talk to him about this. We have to explain that pornography has nothing to do with sex in actual relationships, or with the pleasure adults share with each other. We have to tell him that it's a fantasy. That—"

"And are you going to be the one telling him all this?" Sebastian cuts her off. "Without blushing?"

Marie hesitates before answering. "We've never spoken about it, you and I, but . . . have you watched pornos?"

"Well, yeah, like a lot of teens I watched one or two with friends. Cassettes," Sebastian says, doing his best to appear casual. "There was no internet then. You?"

Marie fiddles with the packet of sugar that she left on the side of her saucer.

"No. What's it like?"

"Lame."

"If it's lame, why do people watch the stuff?"

Sebastian shrugs. Around them, waiters are clearing the tables.

47

"I have another idea, Marie. Lucas is a good kid. He's great with Cuddles. Has always been responsible. What we need to do is empower him. Put everything on the table. Do you remember the documentary we watched on TV not long ago?"

"Do you mean the one by the porn actress who blew the whistle on industry practices?"

"That's it. That's the one. I thought it was a good documentary."

"What's your idea?"

Sebastian takes a swig of his beer. A foam mustache sticks to the down above his upper lip. He puts his glass on the table and licks the bitter foam off with his tongue.

"We treat him like an adult. Instead of lecturing him, we could replay the documentary and talk about it afterward. Not make a big deal out of it."

Marie rubs at an imaginary stain on her cup.

"I guess we'd avoid a lot of awkwardness," she says. "Maybe you're right. But promise me that if that doesn't work, whether he wants to or not, we'll take him for a consultation. His behavior isn't normal."

Sebastian puts his hand out again, palm up, as if to seal a pact.

"Let's do that and see where it goes," he agrees. "We want our son to deal with this."

14

That afternoon, when Lucas gets home from school, nothing happens at first. It's like any other day. Cuddles greets him with purrs and rubs himself around his legs, and Lucas changes the cat's litter box. Then his parents return from work at the same time, around six-thirty. Usually his mom arrives first. His father never before seven-thirty. Lucas doesn't think anything of it, especially as his dad knocks on his door and calls out a casual "hello." For a moment, he paces his room, not daring to go downstairs. He tells himself that his father's coworkers must not have been able to get his laptop or phone up and running, otherwise Sebastian would have already gone ballistic. Relieved, he goes to join his parents downstairs. Marie is busy preparing a salad. He gives her a quick kiss and mumbles a vague "Hi, Mom" before opening the fridge door to get a Coke.

"You shouldn't drink so much of that stuff," his mother says behind his back.

Things are exactly as usual, he thinks. He daydreams

about the moment when he'll be able to reconnect. He's in a hurry now that the danger seems to have passed. He's getting off scot-free. They'll buy him a new phone, a new PC, and it will be over. They eat dinner without mentioning Lucas's computer woes and Lucas helps to clear the table.

"How about watching something on TV with us?" his father asks him, sounding strangely impersonal. "I downloaded it today."

A warning bell goes off in Lucas's head. At the same time, he tries to persuade himself that his father's invitation has nothing to do with the content on his hard drive. It can't be that. His father would never have taken this approach.

"I have an exam tomorrow," Lucas mumbles. "I should study some."

Without responding, Sebastian connects the family PC to the flat-screen TV like he does every time they watch a movie. His mother is already sitting on the couch. Lucas notices the tension on her face. She doesn't look like someone who's about to look at an episode of her favorite series.

"Well, huh . . . I'm going up, then," Lucas says to them.

"No, you're staying."

Sebastian's unequivocal tone tells him that it's pointless to argue. Suddenly, his throat dries up. He skates along the tiled floor until he reaches an armchair and plops down into it. It's near the sofa.

"Have you ever watched an X-rated film?" his father asks him, sounding detached.

What's going on? He can't possibly be about to watch a

porn flick with his parents! He sighs, clearly on edge, hoping he won't have to answer as a title appears on the screen: *Pornocracy: The New Sex Multinationals*. Feeling increasingly ill at ease, Lucas starts fidgeting in his seat.

"Why are you showing me this?" he asks cautiously.

Sebastian dims the lights, as if to avoid meeting Lucas's eyes, and takes a seat next to Marie on the couch. He doesn't answer.

The next hour proves to be one of the most trying in Lucas's life. Deep down he always knew that many of the scenes were staged, totally fake, but he would never have imagined *this*.

This is a documentary on the working conditions of young women who are porn actresses. A string of testimonials that turns his stomach upside-down. Super-gross things that he doesn't want to hear, let alone know about. It's obvious that someone at his father's office managed to open his hard drive. Otherwise he can't see why his parents would inflict such a litany of horrors on him. The enemas, and the vomiting, the physical blows. The split lips and other horrific medical and self-administered numbing agents so powerful scenes are possible to film. The houses where the underpaid actresses from Eastern Europe are confined. The abuse of anti-inflammatories. Girls who've been watching porn since age eight and who film with actors they watched when they were still little girls. The interviews are one thing. The statistics are quite another. More than a hundred billion pages of porn are opened each year online. That means fourteen pages per human being on earth, which includes babies and old people. Suddenly, Lucas feels like he's a drop of water in the middle of the ocean. His small, sheltered world crumbles.

When Sebastian switches the light on, Lucas finds it difficult to control the flow of bile coming up his throat.

"So?" his father asks.

Lucas stares fixedly at his sneakers. He would like for the Earth to split open. He would like to vanish. He would like to die. To be dead. To no longer hear, see, or bear the weight of shame that invades his every pore. He doesn't know what he can possibly say. His mother doesn't say a word either, just sits watching him.

To break the silence, his father launches into a monologue:

"Well, Lucas, I don't need to tell you that Jerome opened your PC and your Samsung. You already know that. And you know that we know. No need to talk about it, but we wanted you to see this documentary so that you're aware of what happens to these poor girls. You get it now, right? You realize what they have to put up with? It's all totally fake and it's revolting as well. Is this registering, Lucas?"

Without lifting his head, Lucas nods with his chin. He feels a tear fall down his cheek. He wants to get up, badly, to run away. He wants this to stop, and fast, and to be left in peace. But Sebastian continues to harangue him, again and again, hammering into him like a nail in a coffin.

"And the photo of you naked, what was it for?"

Lucas stops breathing, like he's got a fish bone stuck in his throat. He can't answer, not in front of his mother.

"What was it for?" repeats his father.

In the prolonged silence that follows, Lucas hears himself mumble, "A girl."

Sebastian cups a hand to his ear. "I didn't hear that, Lucas. What did you say?"

"It was for a girl at school," he says, barely any louder.

"Damn it! I can't believe it!" His father explodes, getting up to pace the room.

Finally, Marie speaks up.

"That's enough, Seb. I think Lucas got the point. Right, Lucas? Do you understand that you've done something stupid?"

Lucas nods as he sniffles. Marie reaches out a hand and rests it gently on his cheek. Lucas recoils as if she's just burned him.

"Look, he's shaken. I don't think he'll start with that again, Seb. I think he's gained an awareness of things."

"I just don't get how you could have spent years at it," Sebastian says.

"Leave him alone now," Marie pleads.

Seizing the opening, Lucas leaps from the armchair.

"Stay put, Lucas, please. We haven't finished."

But Lucas ignores his father's order and rushes to the staircase in desperation. He keeps his focus on the open door of his bedroom, which seems to be farther and farther away with each stair he climbs, his heart beating like a tight fist in his chest. As he plunges into the reassuring obscurity of the hallway, he finally inhales a gulp of air, slams his bedroom door shut with his foot, and throws himself onto the bed, sobbing. Cuddles comes over purring and rubs his whiskers against Lucas's moist cheeks. A moment later, Lucas recognizes his mother's footsteps in the hallway and hears her come to a stop outside his door. She taps it with her fingers.

"Lucas?" she says softly.

He doesn't respond. Doesn't move. After what seems like an endless amount of time, she walks off and Lucas falls into a deep, dense slumber as if submerged under a tide of molten tar.

15

Marie walks off with regrets. As she goes into the bathroom, the soles of her slippers scrape against the floor. She takes a long shower, like she's trying to wash off lots of mud. When she enters her bedroom, Sebastian is already under the covers. She shivers as she slips between the sheets and puts her icy feet on him.

"Ohhh! How can you have such cold feet after showering?" he yelps, burrowing deeper into the bed and laughing.

"Do you think we got through to him?" Marie asks.

"You saw how ashamed he was. I think it was a good lesson."

"Even so, are you sure we shouldn't talk to Dr. Ducros?" Marie insists.

Julien Ducros is their new family doctor. It paid to move and change physicians. The one in Bagneux was as old and incompetent as the new one is young and up-to-date on the latest medical developments.

"Listen, Marie, Lucas is just a teenager who's a little lost, who eats too much, who doesn't exert himself physically, and who spends too much time on the internet. There are millions like him."

"Do you means millions who watch porn all day long?"

"That or other stuff—online games or what not. What he needs is a girlfriend."

Marie shifts her body. "Maybe. But it doesn't prevent depression, something I know about. And we both noticed how much weight he's put on."

"Lucas isn't depressed, Marie. It's not hereditary."

"You don't know that and neither do I."

Sebastian props himself up on one elbow and turns to Marie. "Stop being afraid. Stop feeling guilty," he tells her. "You know what we're going to do? We're going to give him back his devices. Jerome cleaned them up. We should have installed a super-sturdy parental control on his computer a lot earlier. Something like Xooloo."

"Can't we still do that?"

"Marie, he's sixteen!" Sebastian answers brusquely.

Marie feels stupid. She frowns. "I don't care! We could still give it a try."

"It's not realistic."

"A parental control isn't realistic, consulting a doctor isn't worth it . . . everything I suggest is no good. It seems only you know what to do."

• • •

When the judge will ask Sebastian why he objected to taking Lucas to a child psychiatrist, he will remain silent. And when the judge will repeat the question a second and third time, Sebastian will still be unable to formulate the reason for his refusal. He will be unable to explain that he didn't want to start down the same road he had been on with Marie. Because he no longer had the strength. He will also be unable to justify why he forced Lucas to watch a traumatizing documentary on pornography. He will merely explain that he wanted to guilt-trip his son, in hopes of making Lucas reconnect with reality. He will claim that he had not fully grasped the scope and reach of Lucas's addiction.

16

Lucas wakes up with a start in the middle of the night. He dreamed that his parents were chasing him out of the house because Cuddles had been run over by a car—all because he hadn't taken good care of him. He glances around the bedroom for the tomcat but doesn't see him. He calls out to him in a whisper. The house is quiet. Cuddles is not there. He must have gone out through the cat flap Sebastian installed when they moved in. Lucas has always heard that like lionesses, she-cats are the ones who hunt for game to bring back to their den. But in spite of his handicap, and of being a tomcat, Cuddles is a surprisingly good hunter. He usually comes home in the early morning. Still, after his nightmare, Lucas is uneasy. His throat feels parched, like someone poured sand into it. His cheeks burn. He wonders if he has a fever, and then the scene from the previous night plays out in a loop in his mind. He would have liked to waste away. To burn before his parents' eyes. Yes, he would have preferred that a hundred times over to the shame his father inflicted on him.

They will never look at him in the same way. He feels sure his parents will never love him like before. To them, he's become a sex-obsessed maniac. And his father's old friend knows. Soon everyone at his father's workplace will know too. If one of the employees talks about it in front of their son or daughter—a lot of them attend his high school—it's over. He might as well be dead. He tries to free himself from the imaginary cast-iron weight oppressing his chest, but without success. He gets up and gropes his way down to the kitchen without making noise. He opens the fridge door, grabs a bottle of Coke, and gulps down several swallows. The sugar rush that courses through his body offers him relief. He rests his forehead against the fridge door and sighs. He shouldn't have come home. He should have grabbed Cuddles and withdrawn as much money as he could with his bank card and hopped on a train. Never to return. But a train headed where? And to do what? The world around him seems to be shrinking a little more each day since he's been deprived of his devices. He puts the nearly empty bottle back in the fridge door and closes it with his heel. In the dim light he tiptoes out of the kitchen. As he crosses the living room, he notices that the PC is on. Except for special circumstances he is not authorized to use this PC since he crashed his own. And his father changed the password. To log on to the network, Lucas now has to check with him first. Those are the new rules. But after viewing the X-rated actress's documentary last night, in his fury, his father seems to have forgotten to turn it off.

Lucas moves closer to it in the dark. He feels the heaviness of the silence and as if in defiance, he strikes the spacebar. The screen lights up.

His first move is to cut off the sound of the PC. He sits down, opens the browser, and searches the browsing history. His father has not erased anything.

He clicks on the link to the documentary. He's not doing anything wrong, that's what he tells himself, even if he knows all too well where all this is leading. If his father came upon him, he would find him trying to track down information on the documentary, right? That's what he tells himself as he opens the documentary director's Wikipedia page. The filmmaker started out as a well-known porn star in France. Then, according to an article, she became a director of "groundbreaking" porn movies with a feminist bent. *Could there really be some respectable X-rated movies?* Lucas wonders as he clicks on a link that brings him straight to a porn clip. He doesn't quite see how the video is any different from the thousands he's viewed, but he's relieved to find himself in familiar territory. Bits of information from the previous evening float in his mind: *Porn gets 68 million search requests per day. Thirty million people are looking at a porn video at the same time that you are.*

There is one fact that, more than the others, he knows is absolutely true: *Masturbation accounts for only 14 percent of time spent by those who visit porn sites; the remainder is spent searching for the right video to jerk off to.*

Soon, however, Lucas forgets the horrors revealed in

the documentary. Or rather, he wants to forget. In order to think about something else, he lets himself gradually slip toward a compilation of clips, then on to his favorite sites, once again feeling excited and reassured, increasingly hypnotized, at last in the fantasy world he knows so well. It feels good. He can't resolve to abandon his wanderings on the web. Not even when the cat flap opens and Cuddles returns, exhausted from a night on the prowl. Suddenly, he hears the alarm clock go off in his parents' bedroom. He has just enough time to erase his browsing history, put the computer to sleep, and go back upstairs as quietly as possible. In his room, he gets under the bedcovers and waits to hear the familiar noise of the toilet flushing, which signals that his father has gotten up. He's so relieved to have resumed his routine that he falls into a peaceful sleep.

17

Sebastian scratches his belly as he goes downstairs. He notices the power light of the PC is on. Did he forget to turn it off last night? That's not like him. He must have been preoccupied. It was an unpleasant evening. He clicks and the screen lights up. The search engine pops up. Strange. He goes to the browser history. Well, at least he erased it. Suddenly, he realizes that the seat under him is warm. He frowns.

"Lucas?" he shouts.

A meow answers him from above. No need to look further. Cuddles must have settled on the seat before heading upstairs. Sebastian tells himself that he's going to become paranoid. He checks the time on the screen. He'll be late for work if he continues. He turns off the computer, stands up, and heads to the kitchen. Tonight they'll give Lucas back his cell phone and PC. The documentary must have made his son understand how wrong his behavior has been, and he will stop, he thinks as he hurries to get ready for work.

18

Lucas feels like he's facing a tribunal. His parents are seated. His laptop and smartphone are resting on the dining room table. He's standing on the other side of the table, in front of them.

"We aren't going to dwell on this for a hundred years," his father says. "I think you understand. No need to spell things out. We're in agreement, aren't we?"

Lucas looks at his mother, but she avoids eye contact. Evidently, she finds the gray finish of the tabletop a lot more interesting. Lucas doesn't blame her. He wants this to be over with too. He wants to be done with the ceremonial handover of his gear. He can't wait to get it back.

"Jerome cleaned everything up. Your box is like new. He also erased all the junk that you downloaded onto your hard drive. Photos included."

Lucas jumps. "Not Cuddles's photos?"

His father sighs. "Listen, I wasn't about to ask him to sort through all your garbage. You have only yourself to blame. You didn't have to be such an idiot."

Lucas shrugs.

"So we understand each other, then?"

Lucas nods.

Sebastian pushes the devices forward. "In any case, Jerome installed an ultra-strong parental control. There's a whole bunch of stuff you won't be able to access."

Lucas mumbles a barely audible "Okay" before taking his laptop and phone. He thinks his father is bluffing. But maybe not. Just in case, he'll download a new browser without the parental control. The extent to which parents are gullible is crazy. Nonetheless, he tells himself that he's got to stick to the rules for a while. At least, he's got to try. To really try. He knows the whole porn thing is starting to poison his life. And the voices and images from the documentary haunt his thoughts too.

After the incident with the selfie that he sent to Samira, he was already not proud of himself, but now that he knows the dark secrets of the porn video industry, he feels guilty at the idea of going on his usual sites. He begins to think that his father isn't entirely wrong. Maybe if he exercised, he'd lose weight. Maybe if he stopped dozing off in class, his grades would improve. The problem is that even when he's not looking at porn he can't sleep. He twists and turns in bed, drenched in sweat, and has trouble getting to sleep before dawn. Consequently, at school, he nods off anyway.

19

The best resolutions never last very long. Lucas stuck to his resolve less than a week before starting up again. Just like before. Actually, it's worse. It's not difficult to hide. During the day his parents aren't home. Now he's skipping classes to surf the web and only goes to tennis if he knows his mother is picking him up or dropping him off. At night, he goes to bed early on the pretext that he's sleepy. He never turns on the sound. If he hears a noise, like his parents coming up the stairs, he always has time to close the window on his screen. He never connects to more than one porn site at a time, which has the benefit of minimizing the risk of viruses. He doesn't download anything. His laptop seems to be holding up. He still nearly got caught several times because his father no longer knocks on his door before entering. Thankfully, he devised a strategy: he's always got a Wikipedia page about a tennis champion at the ready. He just needs to click on it, and even if he hasn't had time to leave the porn site, it covers up the incriminating page.

He meticulously erases his browser history. But that's basic. So far, so good.

It's not exactly like before. The fear of getting caught has morphed into complete terror at getting caught. And from time to time, images from the dark behind-the-scenes documentary flash through his mind.

He's flooded with guilt by the obscene images and by his desires that are as obscene as the real working conditions of the actresses.

He feels mounting anxiety, tells himself that he's bad, that he shouldn't be doing this, that he needs to stop.

Now the fear of being unable to stop himself from seeking out increasingly violent videos torments him.

The problem is that the only thing that relieves his tension is taking refuge in porn. Here, he's able to let go and forget everything—the tension, the fear, the shame, the guilt, the feeling of dependence, his weight, his failing grades, everything. And each time, as soon as he feels relief, he turns off his screen and promises himself that it will be the last time.

The hardest part is finding time for his homework. Time just slips through his fingers. Lucas doesn't see the hours or the days go by, and even less, the nights. His grades continue to plummet. And he's constantly tired. How many times during his classes has he slumped onto his desk? Since he isn't the only one that happens to, the teachers hardly say anything. Sometimes he wonders if his classmates are dead tired because they spend their nights looking at pornos too. Or maybe some are addicted to other stuff. Apparently, a lot of them are getting to bed late. Are the girls looking at unsavory stuff as well? The very thought turns him on. He imagines a scenario with Margot. He likes her. He wonders if she's already done it. Some of the girls in class must have. He read somewhere that the average age girls first have sex is seventeen. Maybe seventeen and a half. But to obtain that average means that there are younger ones and older ones who've done it. He often thinks about each girl in class, trying to guess which one is most likely to put out. And what about him? According to the report, he isn't far from the average age of a guy's first sexual experience. He's still a virgin! He hasn't even kissed a girl, let alone had sex with one. When he gets to this point in his ruminations he's usually close to turning on his computer or hunkering in a corner to connect his smartphone to a favorite site.

When the school requests that his parents come in for a meeting, he isn't particularly alarmed. He knows it can't be to congratulate them on their son's academic achievements. But there is no way that his teachers can suspect a thing. Neither can his parents. He's been extremely careful. He's sure the school just wants to tell his parents that he's not working hard enough and that he needs to make more of an effort. Of course, he'll promise to do that. And when he makes the promise, he'll believe it. This time, he swears, he'll stop.

20

Lucas and his parents walk down the noisy school hallways, passing by classrooms that ring out with the cries of students. Sebastian left work early and Marie was able to get away too. It was important that they come together, both accompanying Lucas. All three of them wait on a bench outside the principal's office. Sebastian checks emails on his cell phone, while Marie texts coworkers at her office. As he watches them, Lucas thinks, *Guess I'm not the only one who likes screen time.* He takes his smartphone out of the pocket of his sweatpants—which he'd tied low, below his bulging stomach—and connects. Not onto X-rated sites; not here. He'd like to because it calms his nerves, but it's not really possible, so he surfs pages about movie stars. Then Ms. Lacoste comes out of her office, followed by Benjamin, who glances at Lucas as he passes by with his mother. Ms. Lacoste is the principal and she also teaches biology. Students call her the Crocodile, especially those who play tennis, because of the crocodile logo on the Lacoste polos.

Otherwise, there is nothing particularly reptilian about her. In fact, if anyone asked Lucas's opinion, she's super-hot. Even in the sneakers she's wearing this afternoon, instead of her usual high heels.

"Mr. and Mrs. Delveau? Please come in," Ms. Lacoste says in greeting.

. . .

The office is furnished with a desk and three chairs that Ms. Lacoste gestures toward. The chairs are all on one side. Ms. Lacoste lowers herself into an armchair, facing them. A coffee table covered with prevention brochures separates them. Lucas distracts himself by glancing at the various titles—*Radicalization, Dependence, Cannabis, Harassment, School Violence*—but he reads without retaining the words.

He especially avoids raising his head when the Crocodile addresses his parents.

"Things are not going well for Lucas. Can you tell me how he spends his nights?"

Inwardly, Lucas gives a start. She obviously suspects something. But how can she possibly know?

Best not to react. But his father looks at him, surprised.

"Why the question?" his father asks.

"Lucas routinely falls asleep during his classes."

"But he goes to bed early, around ten o'clock at the latest, every night," his mother says, sticking up for him. "I don't understand. Is he the only one?"

The way they're talking about him as if he isn't there makes him bristle, even as he remains poker-faced.

"No, far from it," the Crocodile confirms. "But in Lucas's case it's chronic. And his grades reflect this."

"Maybe he's bored," his mother objects. "Maybe the education at this school isn't suited to our son."

Ms. Lacoste stiffens, on the defensive. She straightens up before answering.

"No, Mrs. Delveau. The education here is top-notch. The graduation rate is very high."

"Surely you know that that doesn't mean anything," his father interjects. "These days, high school diplomas are pretty much given away."

Ms. Lacoste clears her throat before continuing. "We are straying from the reason I called you to this meeting," she says. "It's one thing for Lucas to have poor grades and to sleep through his classes, it's quite another for him to cut classes."

His father's jaw drops. It's Marie who speaks up.

"Excuse me? Are you accusing our son of skipping school?" she asks in disbelief. "With whom, exactly? He doesn't have a lot of friends that I know of!"

"With whom is not my problem, Mrs. Delveau," Ms. Lacoste replies dryly. "It's yours. I'm not accusing your son of anything. I'm relaying facts. Last month, Lucas cut his biology class two times, his English-language and social studies classes three times, plus all of his phys ed, which, given his weight gain, is hardly surprising," she concludes, turning to Lucas.

"Well, don't be stigmatizing!" Marie says, getting worked up.

Sebastian gives his son a scrutinizing glance. "Lucas? Is it true?"

How can Lucas pretend that it's false? Of course he wasn't in class. He's well aware of where he was and what he was doing. It's best not to answer. Or at least to answer as vaguely as possible. He mutters that yes, he cut classes. But when Sebastian insists, when he asks and asks again where Lucas went and with whom, Lucas has a sudden flash of inspiration.

"At home. I stayed home to try and catch up on schoolwork," he says, lowering his head. "I was alone."

"That's nonsense!" the Crocodile says, losing her temper. "Utter nonsense!"

"Are you calling my son a liar?" Marie says, getting equally angry. "I don't give you permission. Just because Lucas is overweight and has poor grades doesn't mean he's a liar. I've told my husband that we should take him to a doctor. It could be that with all the sodas he guzzles he's simply diabetic. Which would explain why he falls asleep in class and—"

"Whatever the reasons may be, Mrs. Delveau, we don't foresee that Lucas will be graduating under these circumstances," Ms. Lacoste interrupts her. "Either he stops cutting classes and falling asleep, and his grades improve, or we will have to hold him back. The rest, as I said before, is yours to deal with. Of course, we're at your disposal if you need advice."

"Advice?" his mother shouts as she gets up. "I would never ask your advice. Don't you understand that Lucas is different?"

"They all are, Mrs. Delveau."

His father is standing as well. He hasn't said anything in a while. He's been watching Lucas closely, sizing him up.

Lucas puts on his parka. He feels his father's firm hand on the back of his neck as it guides him with authority toward the door.

21

As soon as they return home, Lucas shuts himself in his bedroom. He hears his parents arguing about him downstairs. His mom defends him. His father suspects him. She absolutely wants to take him to see a psychiatrist. *She should be the first one going,* Lucas thinks as he opens a site.

He's greeted by a Christmas ad with reindeers, a sleigh, Santa Claus, the "Jingle Bells" tune, and a pinup, and then the menu of the day's videos appears. He skips the seasonal category of orgies where the multiple male partners are decked out in red overcoats and fake white beards, and he chooses *Hentai.* He recently discovered this Japanese-style animated porn. He loves this blend of childhood and sex. And at least these aren't real women, so no one is getting exploited; they're just cartoons. The thing is to find one that hasn't been censored. The Japanese often pixilate intimate body parts. But he finally finds what he wants. Immediately, the onslaught of images soothes him. His anxiety subsides. He even feels less guilt. After all, it's only an animated film. He doesn't hear his parents' ongoing argument anymore. He doesn't hear his father shouting at his mother.

"All the same, tomorrow I'm taking the box in to get it checked. Then I'll have a clear conscience. If he's started up again—"

"Stop accusing him!"

"If he's started up again," Sebastian insists, "I'll take away his computer and his phone until he's legal. It won't be my problem after that."

"If he's back at it, we are taking him to a shrink. Period," Marie says stubbornly.

Sebastian hits one of the couch cushions with his fist. "Stop defending him, Marie! Sometimes I wonder if you're the one who shouldn't be going back to the psychiatrist."

Marie's had enough. She goes upstairs and shuts herself in the bathroom. As she looks at her reflection in the mirror, she notices bags under her eyes and shrugs. She opens the medicine cabinet and swallows a sleeping pill. *Just one to sleep,* she tells herself. Then she steps into the shower. With her hair wet, she staggers to her empty bed. She can just make out the soundtrack of a video game and recognizes that it's *Grand Theft Auto.* Sebastian is addicted to it, claims that it relaxes him. She slips between the sheets and her damp blond hair outlines a ring on the pillowcase. Finally, she closes her eyes.

Lucas doesn't see any of this. He's presently mesmerized by a savage sex scene between a woman who's tied up and a phantasmagoric monster. Soon bored, he clicks on a link that lands him on a site specializing in things he never knew existed.

22

The noise of the balls bouncing on the courts is amplified by the height of the dome.

Lucas continues to cut tennis every chance he can—every time his mom doesn't force him into the car so she can drive him over. Unlike school, no one here alerts parents if you're a no-show. He says he's walking over, that it's not far, especially since his mother has forbidden him from climbing aboard Benjamin's scooter. It doesn't bother Lucas to disobey, but Marie is unaware that Benjamin no longer wants to give Lucas a lift.

"You're too fat, butterball, you're going to tip us over," Benjamin told him a few weeks ago, when Lucas wanted to catch a ride home with him.

At the moment, Benjamin faces him on the opposite side of the court, where he serves for the set. His lean body stretches up toward the dome; he tosses the ball and hits it with his racket and lets out a grunt. Lucas pants as he runs. Drenched in sweat, he goes to the net in slow motion and, of course, misses the return. It's the third consecutive time. He breathes out of his mouth, doubles over, his hands on his knees. A line of drool runs down his chin.

"Delveau, what are you up to?" shouts Mr. Stepanovic, the tennis teacher. "Get back in place!"

Lucas straightens up and pulls at the soaked polo top that clings to his exhausted body.

In three strides Benjamin reaches the bleachers where his friends, a bunch of guys, all of them reed-thin and decked out in white Sergio Tacchini sweats, are cheering him on.

Benjamin bends over the railing and whispers to them. They all turn to Lucas and howl with laughter. Slowly, Benjamin walks back to the center of the court, picks up a ball, gathers his momentum, and aims. The ball hits Lucas on the face. He cries out in pain and doubles over, holding his right eye. Then he collapses.

"Lucas, are you okay?"

Mr. Stepanovic is bending over him. He gently yet firmly removes Lucas's hand from his face. The ball hit the cheekbone, which is already beginning to swell. A few more centimeters and it would have been the eye. Benjamin's friends are guffawing. The teacher helps Lucas up as one of the boys shouts out, "Fatso stinks!" Benjamin can hardly hide his smile. Mr. Stepanovic walks toward him decisively, skirts the net, and plants himself in front of his face.

"I can't prove that you did that on purpose, Benjamin," he says, looming over Benjamin by a good six inches. "But I want you and your buddies out of here."

"But, sir—"

"No 'but's. Get out! I don't want to see you until next week. If this happens again, you're expelled. Permanently." He turns to Lucas. "That's enough for today, Lucas. Go home. Stop by the infirmary first and get some ice."

Lucas thinks that this time, at least, he won't have to lie. He definitely went to tennis. He can prove it.

23

ONE WEEK LATER

Marie and Sebastian haven't had such a heated argument in years. In fact, it could be that they've never had one as bad as this afternoon. The day after meeting with Ms. Lacoste, Sebastian disconnected the router as soon as Lucas left for school. He loaded it into the car so that Jerome could check what was on it. Sebastian knows it's easy to erase one's browsing history but that the router keeps a traffic log of every connection.

Before the end of the morning, the router had spoken. Sebastian now knows what Lucas is up to when he cuts classes. He wasn't lying; he's been staying home. But not to catch up on schoolwork. He spends his days in front of porn flicks, sadomasochist mangas that feature prepubescent Lolitas. Sebastian asked Jerome to reinitialize the router, called Marie, and took the afternoon off. They met at the same café as last time.

"He disgusts me," Sebastian told her. "He makes me want to puke. He's a pig."

"How can you say such a thing? He's your son. He's a child."

"No, Marie, he'll be eighteen in two years."

"Okay, he's a teenager, but he needs help. This time we have to get professional advice."

Sebastian grips the edge of the table. Marie notices that his knuckles are turning white.

"Where did we go wrong?" Sebastian wants to know.

Marie takes her husband's clenched hands in her small palms. "Stop it, Seb. We're going to find a good child psychiatrist."

Sebastian lowers his head. When he looks up again, he stares fixedly at Marie.

"What then? It's all bullshit! No more computer. No more internet connection. We'll change the password to the router and we won't give him access. I'll take away his cell phone too. We're going to tighten the screws on him. We're going to make sure he shows up at school every day. And we're going to force him to exercise. No more being nice and indulgent. Believe me."

Sebastian throws money on the table and stands up abruptly.

Marie hurries after him. With his head hunched into his shoulders like a boxer cornered in the ropes, he stuffs his hands in his pockets, and Marie slips her arm through his elbow.

"You know, it really helped me to see a shrink," she says softly.

Sebastian turns toward her. When he starts to shout, the words hurl from his mouth like flames from a furnace.

"What! What are you talking about? You say any old thing! Is it because the shrink took you off the meds? Because it finally gave me a break? Because thanks to him, you were finally able to care for Lucas when he was little? Is that it?"

Marie lets go of his arm and looks at him like he's a stranger. She opens her mouth to answer but nothing comes out. Not even a breath. She leaves him standing there and takes off in staggered steps toward her car, her heels striking the pavement.

"That's it, just clear off!" Sebastian shouts after her. "It's what you do best, after all. Always fleeing reality."

He walks a little ways. He sees a bar and enters. He orders a whiskey. A double that he gulps down in one shot. He slams the bottom of the empty glass on the counter.

Screw it! Marie can take Lucas to a shrink for all he cares! He doesn't give a damn!

24

Later, in the investigative judge's chamber, Sebastian will explain that he failed to register the impact of the withdrawal.

Lucas had come home from school and tried to go on the internet. The router had refused his password. He had gone downstairs to ask why he wasn't able to connect.

"You're not getting the password." his father had answered. "Hand over your laptop and your smartphone this instant."

Lucas turned and hurried toward his room, but his father beat him to it. By the time he got there, Lucas was out of breath and Sebastian had already grabbed the computer that Lucas now desperately tried to wrestle away from him.

"Stop, please!" Lucas had begged as father and son did a strange dance around the room.

Lucas lunged and didn't see that he'd stepped on Cuddles's front paw, causing the cat to let out a piercing yelp. In turn, Lucas had jumped and released his grip on the laptop, sending Sebastian toppling back from the sudden lack of tension. He had the computer in his hands and he looked at it with a triumphant smile. Tucking it securely under his left arm, he put his right hand out.

"Your smartphone, now."

Vanquished, Lucas had obeyed.

Sebastian admits having underestimated the effects of his son's withdrawal when Lucas subsequently went mute. He confesses to having downplayed the bouts of the shakes that took hold of Lucas in the following days, whenever Lucas sat down for family meals without bothering to touch what was on his plate.

"He's heavy enough as it is; it doesn't matter if he doesn't eat," he told his wife when she pleaded with Lucas to swallow some food.

He admits not having paid attention to the fact that Lucas was sweating and that his breathing was labored. He simply attributed it to his son being overweight. He acknowledges, as does Marie, having overlooked that their son was practically not sleeping, neither at night nor in class. How could they have known, they argue, since Lucas had ceased to communicate with them?

"Still, you finally realized something was terribly wrong since you agreed that he should see a child psychiatrist, no?" the judge asks. He pauses, then continues, "And the high school principal ... Ms. ..."

He shuffles the papers of the file in front of him, trying to locate the name.

"Ms. Lacoste," Marie says.

"Yes, that's it. Ms. Lacoste. She should have flagged the problem and sent Lucas to the school psychologist."

Marie snickers, causing the judge to give her a startled look.

"What is so amusing?"

"There is no psychologist at that high school."

Embarrassed, the judge sets on another course.

"And why Paris? Why head to Paris to see a child psychiatrist? There are quite a few in Chartres that I'm aware of."

"Yes, but we don't know any of them. The one we were going to consult was recommended by one of my coworkers," Marie answers. "He treated her nephew for panic attacks after he quit taking marijuana. We wanted a really good doctor."

"That's the truth. I agreed with my wife," Sebastian pipes up. "We scheduled an appointment for the following week. We told Lucas, and on the day of the meeting, we put him in the car. He was like a lump, not reacting at all. I remember thinking that he smelled bad. I asked him when he had last showered and all I got in reply was a slight shrug."

Marie confirms that Lucas stank up the car, that it smelled as if they'd picked up a homeless hitchhiker. At the house, she had never realized how awful he smelled. She aired out the place frequently, and the rooms were large.

"Didn't you hug your son anymore?" the judge inquires.

I wasn't paying attention, Marie thinks. *Not enough attention.*

"Lucas had become distant" is the only reasonable response the judge gets out of Lucas's parents as to why, when they reached the highway and the car was going at a speed of seventy miles per hour, Lucas suddenly opened the rear right-side door and jumped out.

TURNING POINT

25

Marie is driving and peers into the rearview mirror. In one glance she takes in the empty backseat and, farther off, her son's body bouncing off the asphalt.

"Lucas!" she cries out. "No!"

Her cry gets lost in the rush of wind that invades the passenger compartment. The door beats against the body of the vehicle for a second, and then the wind and speed slam it shut. A brief, strange silence returns inside the car.

"Stop!"

Sebastian's command is unnecessary. Marie has already slammed her foot on the brake. She didn't even look to see if there was a car behind them. She hears other cars skidding as they swerve, brake, and honk furiously, without really hearing anything at all.

"Pull over!" Sebastian shouts. "Pull over!"

Instinctually, Marie falls back onto the emergency lane as Sebastian opens the passenger door before the car comes to a full stop. Without waiting, he bolts from the vehicle.

Several other cars have stopped behind Lucas's still body, which is spread across the right lane some hundred meters back. Another motorist is the first one to rush over. In the left lane, trucks are passing and honking. For a few seconds, Marie remains paralyzed, gripping the steering wheel. This isn't possible. This can't be happening. In a fury, she unbuckles her seat belt and leaps out of the car, a bitter taste in her mouth, and runs after Sebastian, who has almost reached Lucas, whose body a man is already bent over. Behind the man, someone else is taking out a cell phone.

As Sebastian runs the last few meters, his legs feel as if they're glued to the tar from which he must extract himself with each step, and in his head he repeats, *No, no, no, no, no, no, no, no.* At last, he's by Lucas's side, but his brain has short-circuited. He has simply stopped thinking. He bends over his son's body without hearing himself cry out his name, or hearing Marie's cries as she arrives. He hears nothing but his own furious heartbeat, even as he searches for Lucas's with the palm of his hand. Lucas's right leg seems connected to his pelvis at a bizarre angle. His head lies in a pool of blood that spreads out behind his skull. His eyes are closed. He's unconscious. Sebastian lowers his ear to Lucas's mouth. The fact that he no longer registers the tumult around him allows him to grasp Lucas's tenuous and irregular breathing. Lucas is breathing. It's labored, but he's breathing. Fast, fast!

The motorist who called for an ambulance is still talking on his cell phone and Sebastian knows that help is on the way. It will be here quickly, which is what he tries to tell Marie, but she's screaming, so he attempts to calm her.

"Hold his hand and don't let go!" he orders so that she'll have something to do, something useful. "Talk to him and hold his hand!"

He doesn't feel the first drops of rain that plop down on his face. Someone brings an emergency blanket and covers Lucas in a silver shroud. *My God, he's so pale,* Sebastian thinks as his brain begins to function again. He takes hold of Lucas's other hand as someone behind him says:

"Don't move him. It's important not to move him."

A distant wail of sirens finally grows nearer.

26

"It's a miracle," Marie says again as she lies in a heap in a chair.

"A damned miracle," agrees Sebastian, who's sitting next to her, both of them facing the judge. Sebastian's eyes wander and follow a flight of pigeons in the gray sky outside the window until the birds merge into the clouds, then land on the zinc roof of a nearby cathedral.

The judge is short, with fine hair that lies plastered to his head. His lips are thin. He wears round steel-framed eyeglasses, and though he is narrow-shouldered, his blue jacket looks a little tight on him. *He's younger than I am*, Sebastian thinks, *but he looks so much older that it's like he was born old.*

"Are you listening to me, Mr. Delveau?"

"Huh, yes, sorry, can you repeat the question?"

"I was asking why you didn't activate the child lock on the rear doors of your car."

"But . . . Lucas is sixteen!"

A court clerk takes notes on everything that is said. Sebastian's reply hangs in the air in a heavy silence. The judge, whose name Sebastian has already forgotten, nods.

Lucas fell on his side. He sustained multiple fractures to his right leg and pelvis. His head hit the ground only after he slid a good way. He suffered head trauma. The emergency medical services arrived quickly, followed by the police, who promptly realized that Lucas had not fallen out of the car by accident. Marie and Sebastian were so devastated that they did not try to deny this when Lieutenant Peretti asked them if that was what had happened. The officer leaned over Lucas and noticed his black-and-blue cheekbone.

"Is that an older bruise?" he asked, turning toward Sebastian.

Marie didn't give him time to respond. "It's your fault!" she started to shout. "You and your stubbornness! It's all because of you! Why did you refuse to take him to a shrink? Why?"

As she came closer, Sebastian pushed her back. "If you hadn't forced him he would never have climbed into the car and this would never have happened!" he yelled at her.

Lieutenant Peretti took down the Delveaus' heated statement to write up his report, and explained that they would be summoned at a later date to give a detailed account of the incident under calmer circumstances, but what was important for now was that Lucas get the care he needed.

Lucas was transported by helicopter to the hospital in

Chartres. He had already regained consciousness upon arriving but did not remember what had happened. Fearing cerebral swelling, the doctors were reluctant to give him sedatives against the pain.

When Lieutenant Peretti asked about the bruise on Lucas's right cheek, he didn't get a clear response from either parent because they were too busy blaming each other for what had happened. He had seen similar situations before. Situations in which kids and teenagers were abused. Regularly hit. Did the blow that happened prior to the accident indicate abuse? Had Lucas jumped out of his parents' moving car to escape violence at the hands of one or the other? Unsure, Lieutenant Peretti decided to write up a report that he forwarded to the prosecutor in Chartres. The prosecutor hesitated at length between sending the case file on to an investigative judge and filing it without further action. For several years now, cases involving child abuse had been treated seriously. He couldn't risk any mistakes. If the situation soured, it would cost him dearly. He had no desire to find himself reassigned out in the boondocks. So he decided to be cautious and tasked Rémy Boulay, a young and newly appointed investigative judge, to handle the case.

27

Sebastian and Marie were summoned to appear before Judge Boulay the following week for further questioning. Sebastian's face looks drawn, with circles and bags under his eyes. As for Marie, she's been completely out of it since Lucas tried to . . . No! She doesn't want to even think that her son tried to kill himself. She wants to convince herself that he simply jumped out of the car in a moment of folly, without thinking of the consequences.

With effort, and regularly cutting each other off, Sebastian and Marie each tell the judge how rough the recent months have been with Lucas. About his addiction to online pornography, his ballooning weight, his lack of personal hygiene. About the conflicts. About his increased isolation. About everything prior to the accident, without omitting a thing.

"Accident?" the judge ponders. "I would call it an attempted suicide."

He doesn't look happy, Marie tells herself. The judge

seems to think it was our fault. He thinks we were neglectful parents.

She isn't wrong. Judge Boulay is not happy. He's especially against online porn. This case of a teenager addicted to sex via the internet reminds him of another case he would rather forget. A case that he forwarded to the juvenile courts the month before on the prosecutor's orders. It all started with a woman who simply wanted to warn her son about the dangers of pornography. The boy was in seventh grade. The mom had been unprepared for his answer—that given what happened in the school bathrooms with the girls in his class, he didn't need the internet. When she asked for an explanation, he disclosed that twelve-year-old girls gave fourteen- and fifteen-year-old boys blowjobs in the school bathrooms in exchange for cigarettes and money. Shocked, the mother immediately phoned the school. The girls were called before the principal, who gave them a stern lecture.

"But we see that all the time on the internet," the girls said, surprised. "A blowjob isn't sex!"

The boys were temporarily suspended. Furious at having been ratted on—the principal carelessly let the name of the complaining mother slip out—the boys waited for her son at the end of the school day and beat him up, with blows to the head. He ended up in the emergency room, where an intern on call stitched up the ridges of his eyebrows. The mother filed a complaint. The perpetrators were questioned and ended up before Judge Boulay. It didn't take long before they confessed, relaying more or less the same story the girls did. They didn't see that they had done anything wrong. Nothing more than run-of-the-mill porn. The boys didn't comprehend the seriousness of their actions. And the girls couldn't understand that the incriminating facts amounted to prostitution. The judge was horrified by that case and those teenagers.

And now this latest case.

In truth, the judge doesn't know exactly what to make of it.

"Weren't you the least bit uneasy?" he says, tossing the words out to get a reaction in much the same way a poker player bluffs.

"For months I've been saying that we should take Lucas to see a professional," Marie answers defensively as she gives a furtive glance at her husband.

The judge looks at her pensively, then turns to the father.

"Why didn't you take him?"

This time it's Sebastian who lowers his face. "I didn't think it was necessary," he mumbles.

"Even given your wife's history with depression?"

Sebastian doesn't answer, merely shakes his head as tears fog his eyes.

Judge Boulay can tell that the Delveaus aren't violent parents, that they've probably never laid a hand on Lucas. Instinctually, he knows that the tennis player, Benjamin, whom he will summon along with his parents, will confirm the story of the tennis ball, just as the tennis teacher will. The Delveaus aren't abusive. They've just been absent and in denial. They've just abandoned their son in front of his computer screen. It isn't a criminal offense and therefore does not fall under his authority.

28

Lucas remembers nothing. Or rather, he does. He remembers that he was sitting in the back of his mother's car, a lump growing in his throat. That he started to sweat and that he couldn't breathe. That his hands started to tremble as an image of a butterfly caught in the curtain of the kitchen window overwhelmed him, a butterfly desperately beating its wings toward the light until it fell to the ground from exhaustion, where it beat its wings feebly one last time before dying. Now Lucas is lying in a hospital bed without knowing why he's there, his pelvis and right leg in casts, a bandage wound around his head. He's in pain. He's in pain, all over. He feels like someone beat him with a crowbar. The door opens and a nurse walks in. She seems pretty in his blurred vision. When he sees her close up, she isn't as attractive. But she smiles.

"You've been in an accident," she tells him. "A car accident."

"My parents?" he croaks.

"They're fine. Totally fine," she assures him. "They'll be

here later. The doctor too. Now that you're awake I'm going to give you something for the pain."

She attaches a clear plastic bag to a stand, connects the drip to the IV catheter in his arm. Lucas grimaces.

"Don't tell me you're a wimp?" she says, laughing.

Lucas closes his eyes and tries to conjure images of porn as a bubble of protection.

When he opens his eyes again, his parents are there. Seated on each side of him, they hold his hands. Lucas wonders if he's uniting them or if his heavy body is separating them.

"Oh my darling boy . . . ," Marie says as she looks at him and sniffles.

Sebastian tries to tell him something, but the words stay lodged deep in his throat.

Lucas closes his eyes again.

When he regains consciousness, a hospital aide is trying to plump up his pillow and a man in a white coat stands at the foot of the bed like a statue. Lucas reads his name tag: Dr. Frédéric Yzidée. The man smiles.

"Hello, Lucas. I'm your doctor. Your psychiatric physician."

Lucas stiffens at the word *psychiatric.*

"Can you tell me what you remember about the accident?"

"Nothing," Lucas murmurs. "We were on the highway, that's all."

"I don't mean to be blunt but I have to be. You opened the rear door of the moving car and jumped out."

Lucas doesn't know why but he is not surprised. Not at all. In fact, if he could, he'd do the same thing again.

"Your parents were taking you to see a specialist in Paris." Lucas isn't about to forget that. Not a chance. He moves his head in a nod, which hurts like crazy.

"Do you know why?"

This time Lucas doesn't attempt to move. He simply says, "Yes." Dr. Yzidée sighs and stays silent a moment.

"Lucas, I'm not going to beat around the bush," he finally says. "I'm going to be frank with you."

Lucas is trying hard not to listern.

"You'll be staying here a while. We're going to take care of your body and your mind as well as we can. Your body isn't in great shape. Not only because of the fractures you sustained, but because of your weight. I hope you're listening. You're diabetic, type two. We're going to treat you for that and put you on a special balanced diet, with no added sugars."

Lucas knows what this means. It means vegetables. And he hates vegetables. All vegetables. Except for potatoes, which is what he tells the doctor.

"It won't only be vegetables," Dr. Yzidée answers. "When you leave the hospital, you'll be going to a rehabilitation center in Granville. Then you'll be sent to another center in Saint-Brieuc. All of this will take time, Lucas. But we are going to help you."

MAKE THE HEART POUND

29

Afterward, a haze set in. Afterward, Lucas's memories drowned in a magma, an amorphous mush, a goop of marshmallow.

Afterward, a very long tunnel formed in his mind.

After Dr. Yzidée explained to him that he had tried to commit suicide, Lucas fell into a deeper depression.

After came the antidepressant. He felt that it messed with his brain and turned him into a vegetable with a dribbling chin.

Afterward, he no longer thought about dying because he was no longer thinking at all.

Little by little, the doses were reduced so he could begin the rehabilitation phase.

In rehabilitation, he had a really rough time.

At least he had lost a good deal of weight during his stay in the hospital, which was helpful. They kept him on a strict diet for diabetes and weight loss.

Then in Granville, there is the ocean.

Perched atop a cliff, the rehabilitation center is windswept and misted with salt spray. Lucas encounters lots of people there, all of them shattered by life, all of them suffering from multiple traumas. Like Ahmed, who hit the bottom of a pool when he dove into the shallow end—which Lucas thinks was the world's dumbest mistake—and broke his cervical spine. It's supposedly a frequent occurrence. Ahmed is in a wheel-chair. He probably won't ever walk again without assistance.

If he walks at all.

There's also Moussa. Especially Moussa. All bashed up from a scooter accident. He'd been at Granville for three years. One night when Lucas was feeling particularly blue, Moussa spent half the night trying to cheer him up, telling him how beautiful life is, even though he hadn't been able to hoist himself out of his wheelchair for the last thirty-six months.

Moussa, who was found dead the next day in his room. From an embolism.

Without Moussa, Lucas would have continued to feel sorry for himself. But Moussa's death rattled him. That morn-ing he finally realized that he was far from being the worst one off; he just had to open his eyes and look around him to see the truth of that. He halfheartedly decided to apply himself, whatever the cost. In memory of Moussa. Still, on certain days, he can't help but envy Moussa.

Moussa isn't hurting anymore. Moussa is sleeping qui-etly. Moussa, at least, is rid of his burden.

On other days, Lucas feels ashamed of these thoughts.

It takes six months for Lucas to complete his rehabilitation, but he finally reaches the end.

Until his last living days, he will have a slight limp, but nothing that will prevent him, for example, from playing tennis. Except that he doesn't ever dream of tennis, not now that he's discovered the pool. The pool is completely different. *At least if you don't dive into the shallow end like Ahmed did,* Lucas thought.

It's easy to lose yourself in a pool. No need to concentrate. Like most kids of his generation, Lucas learned to swim in preschool. But he hadn't set foot in a pool for such a long time that he had forgotten the smell of the chlorine and how it stings the eyes, how the water caresses the skin, the noises that echo off the glass partitions and high ceilings. And the showers. Because a swimming pool goes hand in hand with showers. His long-neglected body found pleasure in the drops of water that splashed onto him and in the scent of the shampoo that reminded him of his childhood.

Above all, though, there is the ocean. The ocean—which he dipped into as soon as the weather warmed up, even as it made him shiver. The ocean, which makes everything lighter, especially his bruised body. And the salt on his lips, and the goose bumps on his skin when he gets out of the water—all of it brings back memories of a more innocent time, a time before all the porn videos. Swimming laps is like a form of meditation for Lucas, something rhythmic and hypnotic that allows his mind a chance to escape.

In truth, the worst moment during his time at the center

was when he found himself in the library, smack in front of a computer screen. His mouth went dry. He started to sweat, just like he used to when he was forty pounds heavier and he struggled to move on the tennis court. He had to force his fingers, which were automatically composing his favorite web address, to do something else. But what? He didn't know anymore. Suddenly, he couldn't remember why he was there, what the purpose of his research on the internet was. So he simply sent an email to his parents.

His parents visit him every other weekend. His mother is unwell again. Dr. Ducros put her on sick leave. She plunged into another bout of depression as if she had glommed onto Lucas's inner being, and each visit with her son ends in silence.

His father doesn't know what to say to him either. He and Marie exchange small talk with Lucas, ask about the progress of his rehabilitation, then descend into awkward silence. The only time the visit went well was when his father had the idea to bring Cuddles along in the cat carrier. Instead of heading to the beach the way they usually did, Sebastian led all three of them to the parking lot. As soon as Lucas heard Cuddles's meowing, he broke down in tears. The cat leaped out of the carrier to rub himself against Lucas, purring and lifting his head toward his master, eyes stretched out in slits, and Lucas scooped him into his arms and buried his face in the ball of fur.

"My little Cuddles, my little Cuddles," he repeated over and over.

Saying good-bye was all the harder, and afterward Lucas sank into an especially dark period. But before he parted with his parents, he told them:

"I'd like to come home."

"We'll talk to Dr. Yzidée," his father promised.

• • •

Although Lucas's general condition has improved—he's walking again, and his diabetes and cholesterol levels are normal since a dietician helped him to lose weight and get his body under control—his internal state remains tattered. That's what the psychiatrist explains to Lucas's parents a few days later. Lucas is still fragile and he sleeps poorly unless he pops the sleeping pills he's allowed to take.

If the medical report that the staff at the center forwarded to Dr. Yzidée at the hospital in Chartres is to be believed, Lucas alternates between periods of aphasia and over-excitement. The erratic ups and downs in Lucas's morale worry Dr. Yzidée, who fears that Lucas might have a relapse. At the end of his stay at the rehabilitation center, Lucas is supposed to go home for a brief period before spending three months at a specialized center for teenagers, but given Marie's latest depression, Dr. Yzidée feels it would be best for Lucas to go directly there. He also suggests that Marie and Sebastian enter therapy as well.

Sebastian and Marie both nod in agreement, without so much as looking at one another.

30

The Poseidon looks nothing like what Lucas imagined. It isn't a prison where crazy teenagers get locked up. He can't see the ocean from his bedroom window the way he could at Granville, but when he goes out onto the terrace where teens hooked on cigarettes cluster to smoke, he can smell the sea because it's not too far away. He can also go there on foot as often as he wants. Everyone is free to come and go, at least during the day. And when he takes the path that runs alongside the river below, it doesn't take Lucas more than half an hour at a swift pace to reach the marina.

There aren't a lot of kids at the center, less than forty boys and girls. Each with their own bedroom. No one talks much. At least, that's the impression Lucas has. He's only just arrived, but aside from polite exchanges like "Please pass the bread," or "Pass me the salt," or "Thanks," no one has really spoken to him. The building dates back to 2000 and is clean and quiet, except when a resident blows a fuse, something that happens about once a week. The cafeteria doesn't really look like a cafeteria. It resembles what he imagines the cafeteria of a corporation looks like. More of a dining hall. It's on an upper floor and there are even flower beds. In addition to the small garden, there is a nice view of the ocean, as well as a pool. Lucas looks forward to swimming every day. He told the psychiatrist he met when he arrived the previous day that he didn't know how he would manage without a pool when he went back to Lèves. She pointed out that he had just voiced the possibility of returning home.

"Do you want to go back?" she asked.

Lucas shrugged. "Well, yes, I suppose so."

"Do you miss your parents?"

Lucas avoided the question. "I miss my cat a lot, the house, and . . ."

Clara Desnoyers, the clinical psychologist at Poseidon, didn't push it. In her notes she underlined the fact that Lucas had expressed interest in returning home, which she deemed encouraging. She explained that his time at Poseidon was in no way a punishment. On the contrary, the purpose was to put an end to his addiction using a targeted cognitive and behavioral treatment. Lucas didn't understand a word of her mumbo jumbo, but he was nonetheless glad to learn that although he was meant to stay for three months, he could decide to leave at any time. They talked some more and Dr. Desnoyers confided that she was familiar with his former hometown, Bagneux, because she had lived there when she was a student.

Lucas's rough estimate is that the doctor is around

thirty-something. She's rather pretty, with freckles that spread over a large, flat face further enhanced by red eye-glass frames. Lucas takes in the wool dress that clings to her shapely body, and the black opaque tights that cover her legs. She isn't fooled; he knows it. She's just crossed her legs in a defensive way and placed her folded hands on her knees. A few months ago such an encounter might have aroused him. But not now. Nothing happens. Nothing at all.

31

Luc Flohic, the child psychiatrist who runs the Poseidon, encourages Lucas to join some activities. He's a fan of poetry and knows Dr. Yzidée well. As he explained to Lucas, he and Dr. Yzidée both studied together during their grad work.

The thing is that Lucas isn't interested in much. Poetry? He knows nothing about poetry. Shop class? Nope. Culinary class? Nope. Gardening class? Double nope. Boxing class and what else? As for the information technology class, well, it's probably a good idea to forget computers for now. The last time he came face to face with a computer in Granville, it didn't go too well. He doesn't have any sexual desires, anyway. Maybe it's because of his wretched medications.

He doesn't see what he can possibly do to occupy himself. He feels the onset of boredom looming on the horizon. The only thing he wants is to swim laps in the pool, hour after hour. At least there, he doesn't dwell on things. His thinner body from his time in the hospital and in rehabilitation has become muscular. Whenever he sees his reflection in a mirror he hardly recognizes the lean young man he's become. He hardly recognizes the boy the guys at the tennis club called Fatso. Last night, he heard someone crying in the room next to his. It woke him up. Whoever it was banged their fist on their common wall, which made him jump. This morning he saw a guy dressed in a tracksuit, head covered by a hoodie, coming out of the room. The person looked as thin as Cuddles was when he first found the kitten on the street.

"Is everything okay?" he called out.

The guy turned around and it took a moment for Lucas to register that the scarecrow was in fact a girl. He could barely make out her dark crew cut under the hood when she raised her head. What really caught his attention was the purplish mark under her left eye; it left him wondering if someone had punched her in the face. She isn't tall, and she's so slender that he's reminded of a tree branch in winter. Her watery ice-blue eyes focused on him long enough for him to observe her thin lips, her high cheekbones, her minuscule pupils, and for him to think: *She looks just like a guy!* She didn't answer his question. She just turned around again and disappeared down the hallway, the soles of her red sneakers squeaking with every step on the green linoleum.

32

It's been a week, a week of going round in circles. Lucas attends the weekly Friday gathering at noon, where the culinary class serves a nonalcoholic beverage to accompany some tapas, but it's not enough to fill a week. Not by a long shot. So when Dr. Flohic pounces on him about giving the writing class a try, Lucas finally agrees to go. The doctor invited a poet-in-residence to lead the workshop. Lucas had gone to see Dr. Flohic with the intention of announcing that he wanted to leave Poseidon, but he didn't get the chance. The doctor caught him off guard. Lucas looks around the light-gray-walled office as if searching for a way out. His animal-caught-in-a-trap look doesn't escape Dr. Flohic.

"What is it?" Lucas asks, hoping to score a point. "Slam poetry?"

The doctor laughs. "Nope. Just poetry, that's all."

Writing isn't really Lucas's thing.

"I'm lousy at it," he mumbles. "And I make lots of spelling mistakes."

Behind his glasses and a slight potbelly that gives him a jolly appearance, Dr. Flohic is like a beast and he relies on his instinct. He's sniffed the scent of blood—ink blood—of an appetite for words that lies hidden within Lucas. He's sniffed out a part of Lucas that Lucas doesn't even know exists.

"I don't want to do anything," Lucas grumbles again.

"Don't tell me you're afraid?" Dr. Flohic says to provoke a reaction.

Lucas isn't used to challenges, and even less to being given one.

"Afraid? Afraid of what?" he asks, surprised.

"You're right, that was stupid," Dr. Flohic goes on. "Someone who jumps out of a car going seventy miles per hour isn't afraid of anything, right?"

Lucas looks at the shrink fixedly. The color of Dr. Flohic's eyes reminds him of oysters, which he hates. Without knowing why, he decides to play it straight.

"Maybe I jumped *because* I was afraid," he answers, ill-tempered.

"That's good, Lucas," Dr. Flohic says. "You're making progress. Now tell me, why did you drop by?"

"I'm bored. If I stay here I'm going to die. I'd like to go home."

Dr. Flohic doesn't answer immediately. A *ding* announces that he's just received an email. He goes slowly around to his desk and stands to read the message. He then raises his eyeglasses to his forehead and sighs as he considers Lucas.

"Here's what I propose," he says. "The writing workshop

meets on Mondays. You'll remember that we decided with your parents that you need a complete break. That they wouldn't come to see you here. You're going to be bored through the weekend. And the weather is going to be lousy. At the same time, if you want something to do, the boxing club has a match scheduled for Sunday, and the writing workshop begins on Monday. Why don't you give it a try? If you don't like it, then you can go home. Deal?"

The doctor extends his hand.

Lucas hesitates. He attempts to guess how heavy the shrink's pudgy palm will be.

Then he gives it a weak shake.

"Okay. Deal."

33

The idea of the boxing match doesn't appeal much to Lucas, but he has nothing better to do. And his neighbor, not the girl who looks like a guy but the one across the hall from him, also told him about it after he left the psychiatrist's office yesterday. The guy's name is Édouard and he's from Guingamp, a town not far from Saint-Brieuc. His problem is alcohol. Beer. He started drinking before he turned twelve, up in the bleachers of the town stadium.

"You know, dude, in Guingamp, soccer is sacred. It's a religion!" He starts waving a fist in the air and shouting, "Go Guingamp! Go!"

Despite his crazed-dog look, his bright-checked shirt, his curly poodle hair, and his broken nose, Édouard is pretty likeable. Besides, Lucas has nothing better to do.

So when Édouard knocked on Lucas's door this afternoon, Lucas followed him down to the basement to watch the boxing match. Or, to be precise, the matches. It's Lucas's first time at a boxing event. Half of the forty residents are there. Even some staff members, along with visiting parents who've come to support their champion. The air smells of leather, talc, and sweat. Even though the building is nearly new, the basement feels worn and lived-in. *I guess that's normal for a basement,* thinks Lucas. He doesn't have time to dwell on it more. The fluorescent lights go off, plunging everyone seated on the simple white benches into darkness, while the vertical light splashes on the slightly elevated ring. A referee dressed in white climbs onto the stage—Lucas thinks of it as a "stage"—same as the one he saw when he went to see a play by Molière on a school trip to Chartres. Murmurs ripple through the audience when Dr. Flohic arrives late. He shuffles into the last row. His arrival is distracting. He nods at Lucas as he passes him. Meanwhile, two fighters are now in the ring. In spite of the leather head guard, Lucas recognizes the first boxer. It's José, a Portuguese guy who landed at the center because of an online gambling problem. Lucas sat next to him on his first day in the dining hall.

His opponent is a huge guy with prominent lips due to the protective mouth guard. Lucas doesn't know him.

"I'll explain," Édouard says, leaning in to his ear. "The guy in white is the referee and the other guy is the trainer. The little—"

"José. I've met him. And the other one?"

"The other one is Johnny. Don't know what he's here for. But I do know that José is going to eat dirt."

The referee brings the two opponents' gloved fists together by way of greeting, and then the bell announces the start of the first round of the match.

Johnny immediately pounces on José and pummels him with punches. It's brutal and direct, and though Lucas knows nothing about boxing, he guesses that Johnny's style is unorthodox. But he's efficient. Each punch lands and poor José is pinned against the ropes where all he can do is protect his face with his gloves while his adversary pounds his ribs as if he wants to fell a tree. Each blow is delivered with a loud *shhhhh*. Lucas is glad José is wearing a leather head guard. With great effort, José manages to fend off his opponent by keeping his red gloves close together. Johnny takes a step back. Thrown off balance, José opens his arms—a fatal error. Johnny seizes the opening and lands an uppercut, followed by a hook.

José falls to the ground as the referee starts the count.

"No way he's getting up," Édouard says.

Édouard's right. José concedes before the end of the first round. The boxers quickly hug and leave the ring after Johnny raises his arms and draws an imaginary V in the air.

"It's the girls' turn," Édouard announces.

Lucas is surprised. "Really? Girls box?"

Édouard shrugs. "Yeah, of course. Don't you know?"

Lucas did not know. He was unaware there was even a female world boxing champion, until Édouard tells him. The only women he's seen box did so sluggishly and without much conviction, punching into the void in a porn video.

By the time Édouard finishes talking, two new fighters have replaced the boys in the ring.

"Look, it's Fatou!" Édouard says, excited. "She's been here two months!"

The girl Édouard just pointed out attracts everyone's attention. She's tall and lean, all legs, with satiny dark skin. Her purple leather head guard reveals only her eyes and shiny lips. She's wearing shorts and a matching tank top and, unlike her opponent, fills them out.

"The other girl is Eloise. She's from Angers. Got here more or less at the same time as Fatou. She doesn't stand a chance," Édouard says, adamantly. He gets to his feet and shouts, "Go, Fatouuuu!"

Lucas stays rooted to the bench. He recognizes Eloise as his next-door neighbor and suddenly understands how she got the purple bruise under her left eye.

A flight of black ravens unfurls across her protruding shoulder blades. Another tattoo on her thin forearm spells out *HELL IS EMPTY, ALL THE DEVILS ARE HERE* in capital letters.

She's a boxer. He wonders how she can possibly be one with her spindly legs. They look like matchsticks poking out from her electric-blue shorts. *With her flat chest, she's about as feminine as a pit bull*, thinks Lucas as she suddenly leaps toward Fatou like a she-devil. Fatou's feet are firmly planted on the ground as she takes the pounding full-on. She protects herself by raising her shoulders into her neck, all the while looking for her opponent's weakness and shuffling right and left to dodge the blows.

"She's letting Eloise tire herself out," Édouard predicts. "It's not going to last long, you'll see. Too awesome!"

In fact, Fatou lands a direct punch that makes Eloise wobble just as the bell signals the end of the first round. With her thin arms spread across the ropes, Eloise lets the trainer daub her already swelling cheekbone and puts her mouth guard back in. Her concave chest rises as she breathes in, and at the sound of the bell, it's as if she's catapulted toward the center of the ring. Feeling assured of victory, Fatou steps forward calmly, not expecting the raw bundle of nervous energy that pummels her with blows. And though she finally steps back to protect herself, and though Eloise's punches lack power, her initial right-hand hooks land. Fatou tries to gather herself, her eyesight no doubt clouded by the punches. Still, she doesn't lose confidence and resumes her tactic to tire out her opponent. Eloise's blows start to slow down. She dances on her spindly calves. Then all at once, she seems to defy the laws of gravity and becomes weightless. Her moves become aerial. Fatou is thrown off balance; it's her turn to step up and take charge. The roles reverse. Now she tries to land blows as Eloise dodges and dances around the ring. The crowd whistles in disapproval.

"Go, Fatou!" Édouard shouts. "She's so scared, she's running away!"

Fascinated by the ballet, Lucas says nothing.

Third round. Eloise continues to dance around the ring and Fatou chases after her, hitting into the void. She tries to pin her to the ropes, but each time Eloise darts off like a bird.

Fatou's sides start to heave as her breathing becomes labored. Her skin is covered in beads of sweat that catch the light and fall in a shower. She briefly grips Eloise and pummels her ribs, but Eloise breaks away and starts shuffling around and around the ring again until, in the middle of the fourth round, Fatou begins to slow down. The outcome takes another turn. Fatou's moves are now leaden. Meanwhile, Eloise leaps into the air like a tightrope walker and swoops down on her opponent.

She changes from bird to cat. In a swipe of her claws, she nicks Fatou's chin. Fatou attempts to answer in kind but Eloise keeps her at arm's length with a series of quick jabs, followed by a direct left jab to the shoulder. Thrown off balance, Fatou opens herself up and Eloise rushes in. Her blows aren't powerful, they can't knock out Fatou, but they are quick, sharp, and she unleashes them without letting up.

It's the referee who ends the bout by raising Eloise's arm.

Édouard stays fixed to the bench, his mouth wide open. Only when the lights come on and the girls leave the ring for the locker room does he find his voice.

"I can't believe it!" he says.

Lucas is impressed. He would never have expected that a boxing match could hold his attention. And if someone had mentioned a bout between girls a few months ago, he would probably have gotten aroused, would have come up with lots of erotic scenarios. But nothing doing now. Fatou isn't bad-looking, but it would require a good deal of imagination to picture his next-door neighbor Eloise in a porn scene.

"Do you know what she's here for?" Lucas asks Édouard as they climb the stairs toward the dining hall.

"Who? Fatou? Meth."

"No, the other one."

"No idea. She doesn't talk much. Not with the girls or guys."

34

Even with the medications he's on, Lucas didn't sleep well last night. He wakes up in a foul mood and gets to the writing class late. Four people are already sitting around two adjoining tables in a small conference room. The teacher has drawn the curtains to reduce the glare of the bright sun that drenches the space. The teacher is on the plump side, with a goatee and long salt-and-pepper hair that he pulls back in a bun. He wears a green Irish sweater that is a bit too large on him and that has seen better days.

"Come in, please," he says when Lucas opens the door gingerly.

Lucas notes the kindness in his voice. *Kindness* is the right word. He immediately likes the guy and his crazy appearance, and thinks that he could be his grandfather or a slightly older dad than his own.

"Good timing. We were just going around the table for introductions. We'll start again from zero. I'm Alain Troadec. I'm fifty-eight years old, a poet, and I'm from Vannes."

He points to an empty chair next to him. Lucas takes the seat and spots Eloise's emaciated frame against the light. He's crossed paths with the others in the dining hall but he doesn't know them. Not really. A burly guy in a tracksuit introduces himself as Brice. He explains that he's sixteen and comes from Alençon. Then it's Manon's turn; she's a blue-eyed brunette in an oversized sweater and her somewhat greasy hair falls like a curtain over her face. She's from Lamballe and fifteen. Juliette is next, a chubby redhead with milky-white skin who hails from Mans.

Standing, she's probably no more than five feet tall, thinks Lucas.

Eloise goes next. She speaks with a startlingly deep voice for someone so slight.

"Eloise. Seventeen. Angers."

That's it. It's Lucas's turn but he's busy thinking that Eloise isn't very talkative. Finally, he clears his throat and takes the plunge.

"Lucas, sixteen years old. From Chartres."

"All right," the poet says as he claps his palms together. "We're going to warm up with an exercise called Chinese Portrait. Does anyone know what that is?"

He hands out sheets of paper and pens.

"We did that once in our first year of high school," Manon says. "You have to answer a series of questions to let others know who you are."

"Right," Brice agrees. "Shrinks do that to see what's going on in someone's head."

124

Troadec smiles. "We don't care about that. Think of it as a game. Which it is, you'll see. Grab a paper and pen. The idea is to answer questions honestly and without overthinking. Okay, let's get started. What's your favorite word?"

"Now, that's hard," Juliette says.

Lucas looks at Manon, who's chewing her pen. He hesitates, then writes: *Cuddles.*

"The word you hate?"

Lucas doesn't know. He hates so many words. Tennis. Hospital. Yes, that's it: *Hospital.*

"Your favorite drug?" Troadec goes on in a neutral tone.

Lucas starts to write *Coke* but the poet adds, "Careful. Be honest. We're not here to judge."

Lucas pauses and strikes out what he wrote. *Who cares, after all,* he thinks. He writes down a new word: *Porn.* Strikes it out and decides on another that's just as sincere but less risky: *Internet.*

"Your favorite sound?"

That one is easy. *The purr of a cat.*

"Your least favorite sound?"

Hmmm. Lucas doesn't know. Brice can't stop rocking his plastic chair back, making it squeak, which annoys Lucas and prevents him from concentrating. Say, that's it! *A creaky chair.*

"Your favorite swear word or dirty word?"

Fuck.

"Type of work you don't want to do?"

Easy. *Teacher.*

"How would you want to be reincarnated?"

"How? Don't you mean what we'd like to be reincarnated as?" Brice asks.

Troadec smiles again. "What animal, plant, tree, get it? Be precise. Don't say a bird, because that's just a creature with wings, or a tree, because that's just a trunk with branches. If you say a hummingbird, that's totally different than an eagle. A palm tree and an oak tree are not the same. The precise words are what conjure up images."

Long before the poet finishes his last sentence, Lucas has written something down: *Cat.*

"And if God exists, what would you like to tell him or her when you meet upon your death?"

A long silence full of incomprehension follows this question.

"When some comedian was asked that question," Troadec goes on, "he answered, 'I hope you've got a good reason!'"

He laughs. He's the only one.

Against the glare of the light, it's impossible to see Eloise's expression.

Since he doesn't know what to say, Lucas first writes: *Hello!* Not amazing, but not terrible. Finally, after a little reflection, he revises himself and jots down: *Why?*

"Okay, time to reveal your answers one question at a time. Your favorite word."

For Brice it's *soccer.* Lucas thinks about Édouard, who's a fan of Guingamp. For Juliette it's *cake.* For Manon it's *sailboat.* Nothing startling for now. But Eloise's response takes everyone by surprise—*elf.* Lucas says *Cuddles.*

"Oh, that's cute!" Juliette lets out.

The hated word for three of them is *scab*. Only Lucas and Eloise answer differently, although not by much. There is hardly any difference between *hospital* and *psychiatric hospital*. At least, that's what Lucas tells himself.

Juliette's favorite drug: *chocolate*. For Manon it's *pot*. Brice—*beer*. Eloise—*online games*. Lucas reads his response—*Internet*. Not a word that makes anyone react. Or maybe they're pretending so they don't seem to be judging. The insult word is pretty unanimous—*fuck,* except for Eloise, who reads her word—*dickhead*—defiantly as she looks at the poet. The word, in all its crudeness, echoes in Lucas's head. A long, embarrassed silence settles on the room, until the teacher bursts out laughing.

"Bravo. That's provocative. Great choice. I've never gotten that response before. Next."

Lucas doesn't really listen to the other answers. A slew of obscene images swirl in his head. He jumps up when he hears his name.

"Huh . . . yes?"

"What would you like to be reincarnated as, Lucas?"

"A cat."

He wonders what Eloise will say. He bets on a wolf.

"A sparrow," she says.

Wrong. Is she bruised from yesterday's match? Lost in thought, Lucas stops listening. He can't see her well because of the glare from the window behind her. At noontime, the sparrow yells out to him as she leaves the room.

"See you later, cat!"

When he gets to the dining hall he looks around for her but she isn't there.

He sits at a table, a plate of beets in front of him. He hates beets. He thinks of the writing exercise they completed just before lunch.

"You're going to make a list of everything you want to toss into a fire," Troadec told them. "Careful! Everything you write down will be destroyed forever. Think hard and throw out small things and big things."

With a bunch of addicts like these, it's not going to be difficult, Lucas thought as he compiled his list: *I'm tossing the following into the fire—my browser history, Coke, tennis, my smartphone, my computer.* He paused, wondering if he dared. Then he added, *my father and . . .* He couldn't go further. When they went around the room to read their responses, there weren't many surprises. Manon tossed her crappy barrettes into the fire, Juliette her binge eating, Brice his cans of beer.

But when Eloise's turn came, she began reading in a monotone.

"I *am* the fire. I don't like receiving broken hearts. I don't like receiving sorrow and broken dreams. Be careful before you feed me, for I will reduce everything to ashes."

Lucas noticed the stud piercing on her tongue.

"Wow!" Troadec said. "You turned the exercise inside out like a glove. Brilliant! Way to go, Eloise!"

She did not smile.

35

Brice interrupts Lucas's thoughts when he comes over with his tray.

"Okay to sit here?"

Lucas nods that it's fine.

"So you come from Chartres?" Brice asks.

"Yeah. Well, from Lèves, just next door."

"That's like me. I live in Perseigne, in a housing project right outside Alençon. Do you know it?"

Lucas does not know it. He doesn't really want to talk. After a while, Brice grows tired of carrying the conversation and the small talk comes to an end. Brice focuses on the food on his tray. Lucas hardly touches his. His thoughts rush around in his head. He's eager to get back to the workshop. Eager to crank out words. Eager to let words loose on paper. He's decided to stay. At least for the coming week. Afterward, he'll see.

36

In the afternoon, it's Brice who surprises everyone. Alain Troadec asked the class participants to write up a list of what makes their hearts beat faster. Small and big things, as always. Brice goes first.

"Soccer, beer, fast cars, sex," he says, his voice starting to tremble. "And my son when he smiled at me for the first time."

Damn! thinks Lucas. He does a quick mental calculation. At best, Brice got the mom pregnant when he was fifteen. Lucas looks at the others and knows they're calculating the same thing. Only Troadec remains impassive. Lucas is bothered. He doesn't want to reveal anything more. He could easily have listed what set his heart beating fast when he watched all the porn stuff, but he's trying to get away from all that, so he wrote: *When my computer doesn't start, when my smartphone freezes, if my cat isn't back home when I leave for school.* At the last minute he added: *The ocean. Watching the ocean. I dream of traveling on it.*

He doesn't really listen to how the others respond anymore, not even Eloise. Anyway, he doesn't quite understand what she's talking about when she reads her list: *Getting a reward on CoD makes my heart beat fast, same for dropping in my ranking, or getting upgraded to Prestige 2 Level 17.* Everyone else seems to get it, though. Suddenly he feels like an alien.

At the end of the class he finds himself next to Eloise in the hallway. She hasn't put on her hoodie yet. Close up, her irises are very pale, so washed-out-looking, as if they've been eroded, and they're tiny, no bigger than nail heads. Her prominent cheekbones and scrawniness make her eyes appear even larger, like they've swallowed part of her face.

"Congrats on the boxing match yesterday," Lucas tells her as he bounces from one foot to the other.

The bruise under Eloise's eye, the one he noticed when he first saw her, is nearly gone. But the punch Fatou landed on her still-swollen cheekbone has turned it purple.

Eloise shrugs. "I don't deserve any credit. Fatou is strong but she lacks finesse. She thought she could wear me out and didn't notice I was doing the very same thing to her, that's all."

"What's *CoD*?" Lucas asks.

Eloise widens her eyes. "Damn, where do you come from? *Call of Duty,* don't you know?"

Lucas feels dumb that he didn't think of it.

"The video game? Of course, I'm an idiot!" he says quickly. "Some guys back at school played it. It's a shooting game, right?"

"Yup."

He continues to bop from foot to foot, not knowing what to say and uncertain about asking anything else. Finally, Eloise takes the initiative.

"Are you wondering if that's my problem? Well, it is. At least, partly."

As she turns to head off, Lucas pipes up.

"What are you up to now?"

Eloise stops. "Well, huh, I'm going for a smoke."

"Want to take a walk? I'm tired of being cooped up."

Eloise looks out a window. It's a beautiful afternoon.

She sighs. "I'm tired too. I like the class but I need fresh air. Where do you want to go?"

"How about the ocean?"

Eloise bites her lip as she looks at the large clock in the hallway. It's four thirty. Dinner is early at Poseidon, at seven. But they have time. They only need forty-five minutes to get to the tip of the marina.

37

The wind gets chillier as dusk settles, casting a copper tinge on the waves. The crashing surf batters the granite cliffs that are indifferent to the pounding. Eloise shivers and hunches her shoulders into her neck, a common habit of hers. On the way over, they talked about Troadec. Lucas thinks the poet has a good way with people, a way to make everyone open up. Eloise mentioned Angers, where she lives with her mother and brother. Then they reached the ocean and fell silent as they gazed out at the waves.

"I played a lot of different games before finding MMOR-PGs," she says suddenly as she lets out a puff of nicotine that gets carried off on a wind gust.

"What?" Lucas asks. "What's that?"

"Massively multiplayer online role-playing games," she explains, uttering the words like she's talking to a dimwit. "It's like regular role playing but online, which means a lot of people can play at the same time. Players form connections with each other, we create virtual communities like in real life, and when you don't play, everything still evolves, which makes you want to know what's been happening while you're not connected."

"Got it," Lucas says, without really meaning it.

"I'll explain it to you. For *Call of Duty,* I had an avatar."

Lucas remembers seeing the movie when he was little.

"You mean like in the movie?"

"Yup. Like in *Avatar.* I chose a male avatar. That's how I found out my mom was addicted to the game."

Lucas turns to look at her. The sinking sun gives her cheeks and some strands of her brown hair a saffron color.

"I'll explain. I was constantly thinking about *CoD,* even when I wasn't playing. If twenty-four hours went by before I could log on, I completely stressed out. Even at school I played. I wasn't doing any work in my classes. The only thing that mattered was what was happening in the game. My mom lectured me about it, but since she spent her nights in front of her computer screen, I wasn't about to listen. I thought she was on Facebook, or that she was looking for a guy on Tinder. But nope, that wasn't it. Then the inevitable happened. My school called us in for a meeting. The principal had my brother in one of her classes. He's a year younger than me. At the time, he was in eighth grade and I was in ninth. Anyway, all three of us were sitting out in the hallway, waiting to see the principal."

Eloise stops. She has trouble breathing. A tear runs down her cheek.

"Darned wind," she says, wiping at the tear.

She sniffles as memories rush back to her like a pack of wild dogs freed from a kennel. It's coming on two years.

38

Eloise and her mother are sitting out in the hallway. Nicolas, Eloise's younger brother, sits between them. He didn't want to stay home. Eloise clutches her smartphone. To Nicolas's left, their mom taps on the keyboard of her phone, wearing a headset. He sighs. On the other side of the wall, the principal's high-pitched voice can be heard in the office. Ms. Lemercier is running late. She should have seen them half an hour ago. Nicolas looks at the clock on the wall. *This sucks. Twenty-five to. What is Lemercier doing?* he wonders. He starts fidgeting. He's too warm in his parka. He takes it off. Another five minutes and he's going to split.

He turns toward his mom and tries to take her phone.

"Stop it with that! Enough!" he tells her.

Eloise doesn't look up. With her earphones in, she continues to play on her phone like a crazy person. Their mom maintains a tight grip on her own phone, but Nicolas gives a forceful tug and snatches it out of her hands. The crooked headset atop his mom's head makes her hair look strange, and the cable dangles. As she lets go, Nicolas is caught off guard and drops the iPhone on the ground by Eloise's feet. The screen lights up. Two things happen simultaneously.

Her mouth agape, Eloise stops playing and stares at her mom's phone. She's just unmasked the opponent who's been making her life miserable for weeks by sending NPCs to mess up her LVL—none other than her own mother.

Meanwhile, on the other side of the wall, when Ms. Lemercier hears "Stop it with that! Enough!" she assumes Eloise's mom is admonishing her online-game-addicted daughter. She discovers that it's Nicolas, an excellent student, who was lecturing his mom, and that mother and daughter are equally dependent on their screens.

After the initial minutes of the meeting and during the remainder of the encounter, Eloise and her mom return to their obsessive playing, and the principal has no choice but to address her caustic remarks to Nicolas in the hopes that he'll be able to relay them, or at least inform his father, if anyone even knows where to find him.

39

"That's how I found out that the two of us were in the same mess," Eloise says. "A mess called *Call of Duty*. When we got home, we finally talked. We told Nicolas to do his homework and we made some tea. Now that the truth was out, we swore that we'd never play *CoD* again, even though we'd reached high levels. We sent good-bye messages to our communities—"

"Your levels?" Lucas interrupts.

Eloise bursts out laughing and Lucas realizes it's the first time he's seen her laugh. He likes the way her pale eyes light up. She draws one last puff of her cigarette before flicking it onto the ground.

"Damn it, I should quit smoking too," she says as if talking to herself. "But the shrink says one thing at a time is enough. Still, I know I'd put on weight if I quit, and I sure need to add some pounds." She turns to Lucas. "Can't believe you don't know about levels. You must be from Mars. The better you play, and the more often you play, the higher you score.

It's the way to climb in the standings. There's something fair about it, not like in real life where lots of people kill themselves at work and never get rewarded. That's what *level* means. And you become part of gamer communities—where you communicate, strategize, and catch up on everything that happened while you were logged off. Understand?"

"Yeah, I do," Lucas says.

"When we told the communities that we were bailing, we got put through the wringer. It was hell. The other players swore we'd never be invited back. It's the only time my mom and I were allies. We supported each other and stuck to our promise. We never went back on *CoD*."

Lucas looks up to watch a squawking seagull fly overhead.

"That's great," he says.

"No, it isn't great. We put all the blame on *CoD*. We told ourselves it would be cool to play a different game. That it would be less addictive. We didn't understand that we weren't addicted to *CoD* but to online games in general. We decided to buy *World of Warcraft*. It's a medieval fantasy universe."

"You mean like *Game of Thrones*?"

"At least you know that much!"

Eloise smiles again, her thin lips stretching in a pencil line the color of a blackberry.

"Come on, I'm not completely out of it."

"I was beginning to wonder," she says, giving Lucas a sly

look before coming closer and knocking her shoulder into his arm.

"I'm kidding. It is a little like *Game of Thrones,* only *Game of Thrones* is like *Care Bears* next to *World of Warcraft.* In just a few weeks, we became even more addicted than we had been to *CoD* 'cause we could buy equipment that gave access to restricted gameplay. Those games were off-limits unless you improved your level and were upgraded. It took a lot of time. Quitting the game became increasingly harder because when you quit, everything you worked so hard for—your stats, friends, equipment, throwing an elf—goes up in smoke. My mom and I each played around ninety hours a week. We stayed shut in the apartment. Nicolas stopped getting on our case. He went to school by himself, either cooked for himself or we ordered pizza or burgers, or anything else we could gobble up in twenty minutes so we could go back to the game as fast as we could. Little by little I ate less and less 'cause I felt guilty for stopping play. My mom and I only went out to buy cigarettes. We stopped seeing friends, and when we were in the apartment, we stopped talking, we just played, or we collapsed on the couch for two or three hours when we were dead tired, day or night. My mother didn't go to work anymore. At first, she convinced her doctor that she needed sick leave, but she didn't go back when the sick leave ended. We became no-lifers. It lasted months. Soon we didn't have any money. The little we did have we used to pay the subscriptions."

"Is it expensive?" Lucas asks while thinking that at least the porn he watched was free.

"Not really. It can cost around twenty euros per month. As long as you've got only one, it's okay. We had two. One each. But that wasn't the worst. Because she wasn't working, my mom wasn't paying the rent. We were evicted from the apartment. We lost everything, including the computers. Everything was seized. The school even contacted child welfare services. My mom almost lost her parental rights at that point. The only reason she didn't is because Nicolas and I went to live with my grandma in a small town near Rouen while she got treatment. But going to Rouen ended up being a disaster. It was like a desert. My grandma doesn't even have a computer. Can you believe it? I didn't know what to do with myself. I was going berserk. I started going out with a guy but it didn't last long. He had friends and I couldn't interact with them. I couldn't talk to more than one person at a time, and talking to no one was even better. He complained that I never said anything. If there were more than two people in the room, I immediately wanted to leave. . . . Actually, it wasn't that I wanted to leave but that I *needed* to leave. The noise, living with others, my grandma, my brother, the cramped living space, it was like I'd lived in a bubble for months and every little sound around me got amplified."

Lucas understands only too well. He shivers. It's getting darker.

"The others say you don't talk a lot. Why are you telling me all this now?"

She turns toward him, seemingly lost in thought.

"I'm leaving in a week. Like Troadec says, it's got to come out sometime. We won't be seeing each other again, you and me."

Lucas ponders what to say and looks at the watch Marie recently gave him to replace his phone. He hasn't gotten used to the tight wristband and feels like he's handcuffed to it.

"It's time, want to head back?"

"I'm not hungry, but okay. I'm never very hungry."

"How do you manage to box?"

"Rage, man! Just rage."

It's Lucas's turn to laugh.

They walk side by side. Eloise kicks her red sneaker into a Big Mac wrapper on the sidewalk.

"I completely lost it," she explains. "The shrink said I had a breakdown. I smashed everything at my grandma's place. She called the police and I ended up in the psychiatric hospital in Rouen. Now I'm here."

Silence. Her voice is slightly hoarse when she next says, "And you?"

Lucas doesn't respond. He isn't ready. It's too much for him. He speeds up and starts to limp. Eloise catches up to him and grabs his elbow. He stops.

"You don't have to tell me if you don't want to," she says. "It's not important."

He gets lost in thought as he looks at a can of beer abandoned in the gutter.

"I had a problem with food too," he admits. "Eating too much of it. Sodas more than anything."

She looks at him from head to toe. "You wouldn't know by looking at you."

"It's because of the accident. I lost a lot of weight afterward."

"Accident?"

"Car accident."

"Oh . . ."

"The hospital, the rehabilitation center, the pool . . ." He stops at this half lie.

Sometimes the emptiness terrifies him. Before, all he had to do was get in front of his computer and—ta-da!

Sometimes he thinks he's gotten the short end of the stick.

He doesn't want to talk anymore. Or only to his shrink.

And even then, he has trouble.

40

It's not similar to what Lucas has seen in the movies. He isn't lying on a couch, and the shrink isn't behind him, nodding every so often like a bobble-head dog so as not to appear asleep.

Clara Desnoyers is seated facing him, in her office. It's a modern room, impersonal, about the size of his bedroom in Lèves, with a stupid plaster Buddha on a shelf for a Zen look, and lots of books.

Lucas hasn't unclenched his teeth since he entered the office. He simply took an inventory of the space, letting his eyes wander from one object to another.

"You mustn't feel guilty for what happened, Lucas," Dr. Desnoyers says, breaking the silence. "I'm not here to judge you, I'm here to help you. Is it because I'm a woman that you don't want to talk? Would it be easier with a man?"

"Maybe. I don't know," Lucas grumbles.

Dr. Desnoyers uncrosses her arms and legs and bends closer.

"And what if I told you that it isn't just a problem that guys have?"

Lucas stares at her in disbelief. "Do you mean there are chicks, huh, I mean, girls with the same problem? Girls who are hooked on pornos?"

The doctor smiles at him, revealing perfectly aligned teeth. Her expression remains sorrowful.

"Well, the majority are boys. But those who view massive amounts of porn aren't all perverts. They're just stuck in the virtual world. I had a young woman who became a cybersex addict at the age of sixteen. She started watching it out of curiosity, reasoning that she was doing what everyone else was. She continued out of boredom. Little by little, she withdrew from the world, almost without realizing it. She too was ashamed. A boyfriend got her to watch the first films, but they broke up when she could no longer make love to him. She hardly knew who she was anymore. Her sexuality had been taken over by the web."

"Just like that?" Lucas asks, finally curious.

"Sexuality rests on three elements: libido, desire, arousal."

Doubtful, Lucas scratches an imaginary zit on his cheek.

"I don't really see the difference," he says. "Aren't they pretty much the same?"

"You get aroused when you watch a video, right?"

Feeling uncomfortable, Lucas shifts from one butt cheek to the other.

"Well . . ." He hesitates, feeling he's on a slippery slope.

"It's normal, Lucas. Pornography relies on that: arousal. It's the goal. The pleasure attached to masturbation is first and foremost connected to arousal."

This time Lucas furrows his brow.

"Do you mean I'm addicted to masturbation? Is that possible?" he wants to know.

"Of course it's possible, Lucas. From a strictly medical viewpoint, we could diagnose your condition as an addiction to sex *via* cyber-assisted masturbation."

"It's bad to masturbate, I know."

Dr. Desnoyers laughs. "Of course it isn't if you're not addicted," she says. "It's not bad at all. Someone who drinks a glass of alcohol from time to time isn't an alcoholic. Same for online games or anything else. It can be nice. But knowing what you like and how to manage it are both indispensable in order to set limits."

Lucas thinks about the doctor's response before asking, "How many times a day is normal?"

"It doesn't work that way." Dr. Desnoyers shakes her head, her loose hair brushing her shoulders. "It's not like there's a national average. It's different for everyone. Each person has a different sex drive. It's just that when it takes over your days and nights, and you do nothing but that, it begins to be a problem."

Lucas gives a sarcastic laugh. "If only it were just one problem! What about desire and the other thing you said?"

"Libido? The libido is something else—it's a person's sexual energy. And desire is something that gets focused on someone. Someone who really exists."

For the first time in months, Lucas thinks about Samira, the girl he sent his nude selfie to.

"Real people frighten me," he admits.

"You told me that you've never had sex with a girl, right?"

Lucas nods.

"You'll understand better when you do, but roughly, since porn only gets someone aroused, the virtual stuff takes over and gradually isolates the viewer. When you're in front of your screen, you're passive. You become dependent without realizing it because you're not ingesting anything, not smoking anything, not buying anything. It's not a drug. It's an addiction with no real product. A virtual addiction. The real product is just a series of pixels, ones and zeros that are coded in HTML."

"The real product is me. What I don't understand is why we get addicted. What is dependence, exactly? And addiction? I mean, what is it scientifically, in my brain?"

Dr. Desnoyers's eyes half close and crow's-feet appear at her temples as she attempts an explanation.

"Every product that causes human beings to become dependent has one common element: it increases the level of available dopamine in a region of the brain called the reward pathway, which is supposed to modulate pleasure."

Lucas digests the information. "So if I'm understanding this, whatever the substance—drugs, alcohol, work, sex, gambling, food, cigarettes—we get addicted to one thing. And that's . . . whatever it is you said."

"Dopamine? Yes, if you like. That's a bit condensed, but yes, humans are addicted to pleasure."

"I don't see anything bad about that."

"Except when it kills you, Lucas. You've got to have a handle on the substance and how to use it."

"Okay. But why, for example, did I become addicted to cybersex? Why wasn't normal life enough for me?"

"Are you asking if there was something missing in your life—some void that you were trying to fill? Is that what you mean?" Dr. Desnoyers asks. "I don't have the answer to that question. You've got to find that out for yourself."

"And . . . the girl you mentioned . . . ," Lucas says, hesitating, "did she find a way out?"

"When I met her she was seriously considering suicide."

Lucas ponders the shrink's response and says, "Like me."

"Like you, yes, but she found a way to get better. And so will you. Today she's married, working, and has two children."

"Cool."

Another moment of silence, and then Lucas speaks up.

"Watching the videos calms me down. It soothes me. At least I'm in control. Not like when I'm with real people." He sighs. "But it destroyed my life. And my parents' lives too."

He sniffles, furiously wipes his wet eyes with his closed fist, and gets up to leave the room.

41

To mark the end of the workshop, Troadec scheduled an additional morning class—just before the weekly Friday social. Lucas isn't in the know, but Dr. Flohic hatched a plan with Troadec and the workshop participants to celebrate Lucas's birthday during the non-cocktail hour. It's a surprise and everyone has kept quiet about it.

The last class exercise consists of an essay inspired from a childhood photo. For the occasion, they received special permission from the center to use the computers. The photos were gathered from the families via email and were printed on paper.

Before the class writes anything, all the photos are passed around the group.

Brice, looking chubby, is laughing in front of a Christmas tree, at the foot of which are piles of presents. Manon stands in front of a sailboat on what seems to be a fishing wharf. She looks to be seven or eight years old. She's wearing a pink one-piece bathing suit and terry-cloth shorts. She's smiling and her two front teeth are missing. An adult who's out of the frame holds her hand. Juliette is at the shoreline of a pond or lake, her bottom in the water, a mustard-yellow sun hat on her head. She's no more than three years old. As for Eloise, she's posing starry-eyed next to a Santa Claus. A stuffed bear dangles from her hand. Impossible to say where the photo was taken.

"Do you remember this?" Lucas asks her.

"I'm not sure," she lies. "I must have been around five."

She snatches Lucas's photo as it comes out of the printer. "Whoa! Too funny!"

Lucas is sprawled in the snow. He just fell down. It's his first time on skis. He's nine years old. His father stands next to him, doubled over with laughter. He's trying to help Lucas up. Lucas remembers this well. His mother snapped the photo. She was back home and feeling better. It was their first winter in the mountains.

When Marie emailed the snapshot, she wrote *I love you* at the end.

Lucas was only able to type one word in response: *Thanks.*

Eloise hands over the photo. He places it in front of him and looks at it. It's hard to connect the happy little boy whose face is smeared with snow with his life today.

Troadec briefs the writers. He seems to know what he's doing.

"Okay, time to begin. You're going to write this essay in two steps. First, you'll describe what you see. Second, what you recollect about the photo. You might not remember anything because you were too young. Doesn't matter. Just tell us which childhood memories surface when you look at the image. When we're done, you'll read your essays out loud. Don't be afraid. It's very possible that you'll be overwhelmed with emotion when you read. No one will hold it against you. If you start crying, well, it's not important. Again, we're not here to judge. We're just sharing."

42

The only sound that can be heard is the scratching of pens on paper, along with the rhythmic gusts of wind that whip against the bay window. Lucas lifts his head from the paper. His thoughts get lost in the seagull he sees fighting against squalls as it allows itself to be carried on the rising air current, its wings outstretched and still.

Lucas never skied again after that initial time. He couldn't stay upright. He preferred the sled, and besides, they never returned to the winter resort. Instead, they would go on summer vacations by the beach. He had nearly forgotten. Still, he vividly remembers that wintertime in the snow, and the memory comes surging back. The smell of the pine trees around the chalet they had rented. The chairlift gently swaying in the breeze as he sat securely bookended by his parents.

He was loved, protected, and snug between them.

He was innocent.

He was unaware of the treasure that was his for a few years more.

That's what he writes. That's what he reads, bravely standing like a little soldier even as his voice cracks and he swallows back tears to get to the end. He sits down. The eyes of the other participants redden.

It's their turn to read. Their words ooze with the nostalgia of childhood, of a former carefree time filled with games, tantrums and insignificant sorrows, candy apples and cotton candy, brightly colored toys and unseemly noises. The nostalgia of that time when what hurt stewed long and deep inside, where what disabled had not yet surfaced in the subconscious. A world supposedly protected by loving adults who they still so much wanted to resemble.

Adults who now, and so often in vain, they do everything not to resemble.

When it's Eloise's turn, she shakes her head vigorously.

"Come on," Troadec encourages her.

But his caring tone implies that he knows she won't read, and he won't insist. He's there to heal, not to inflict pain.

43

Édouard shows up at the gathering. He's wearing a flashy FC Guingamp soccer T-shirt. The cooking workshop baked the cake. The Friday Happy Hour may be alcohol-free, but the glasses filled with green, yellow, and orange fruit juices look inviting. Little paper umbrellas and straws add a decorative touch. Still shaken up by the last writing exercise, Lucas dragged his feet getting to the dining hall.

He never suspected a thing, not even when Édouard shook his hand with a goofy look on his face.

He never suspected a thing—until someone lowered the blinds and shut off the fluorescent lights, and Brice, Manon, Juliette, Eloise, and Édouard were joined by Dr. Flohic, Troadec, and Clara Desnoyers, and all of them surrounded him singing "Happy Birthday," and Fatou, José, and someone named Kevin arrived carrying an enormous strawberry cake topped with seventeen birthday candles, all of them lit.

And then the ground beneath Lucas began to sway. Back home, birthdays weren't cause for much celebration, maybe because of his mother's extended medical absences and all the additional housework his father had to shoulder. They had no close family to help. Lucas never really thought about it before today. What's certain is that he's never celebrated his birthday like this and hasn't blown out any candles since the end of grade school. He can't remember seeing his parents do that for their own birthdays either. The whole thing takes his breath away, and he forces himself to swallow the big lump in his throat so that he can speak and at least thank everyone, and that's about all he can get out as he holds back tears mingled with laughter, and for the first time since coming to Poseidon, there is nowhere else he would rather be. Dr. Flohic has taken out his phone to snap a picture. He smiles and, in a sweeping gesture, invites Lucas to come closer to the cake. A hush descends upon the room, broken ever so slightly by Juliette's nervous giggles.

Lucas inhales a big gulp of air and blows out all seventeen candles in one breath. Everyone claps. The lights come on again. His workshop companions rush to hug him. They've each prepared a short poem on the theme of happiness, another surprise spearheaded by Troadec. The teacher hands Lucas a small wrapped package.

"This is a collection of my poems. Don't feel obligated to read any if you don't want to, but at least check out the dedication. It's a surprise."

Eloise is the only one who hasn't stepped closer. As she draws nearer now, she gives Lucas an envelope.

"For you to read," she tells him.

Then she gives him a hug, just like the others have done, and Lucas feels an electric jolt, something he wasn't expecting. He steps back abruptly. Eloise looks at him.

Something tells Lucas that she also felt the jolt. He knows it by the way she turns away from him with regret.

Music starts to play. Lucas looks around to see who's responsible. It's Dr. Flohic. The bass makes the walls vibrate. Everyone begins dancing, except those who hungrily dig into the cake and drink the fruit juice cocktails.

Lucas lets Manon lead him around the tables and chairs that have been pushed to the side to create a dance floor. Quickly, he scans the room for Eloise but doesn't spot her. His hand still grips the envelope she gave him. He folds it, puts it away in the pocket of his sweats, and gives himself over to the music.

44

The afternoon flies by. One by one, the partygoers go back to their rooms or out on the terrace to smoke. Smoking is frowned upon, but they are allowed to do it. Lucas doesn't see Eloise among them. He approaches her door but does not hear any noise from inside. He doesn't dare knock. He goes into his room and drops his gifts on the bed, then remembers what Troadec had told him: *At least check out the dedication.* He strokes the gray cover, gray like the sea, with his thumb, and makes out the title: *Heartbeat.* He opens the cover to the title page and easily scans the poet's elegant cursive handwriting.

For Lucas, whose heart beats fast for the Atlantic Ocean. Happy birthday!

Troadec had taped a ticket onto the page. Lucas detaches it. It's for an excursion on an old sailboat, in Saint-Quay-Portrieux. He has no idea where the port is located, but his heart does start beating fast. He hopes it's not too far away. Not in the mood to read, he closes the collection. Suddenly he can't stay still. He decides to go back to the dining hall but everyone is long gone. Only the remains of the party are left on the tables.

The residents who go home each weekend are already gathering their belongings.

At loose ends, Lucas thinks about swimming some laps when he feels the envelope he stuffed in his pocket. Eloise's gift.

He abandons the idea of swimming. The soles of his sneakers squeak against the linoleum floor of the hallway as he remembers their quick, awkward hug and the shiver that jolted through his body. He goes to his bedroom again and closes the door. He sits on the edge of his bed and takes the envelope from his pocket. He opens it with care.

The envelope contains two sheets of paper, neatly folded in thirds. The first sheet is the image of Eloise he saw in class earlier in the day, the one of her and her stuffed bear and Santa Claus.

The second sheet is covered in a messy scrawl that slants one way, then another. He has to read some portions twice, but he finally gets to the end.

Of course I remember this photo. I was only five years old, but there is no way I'd ever forget. No way at all. My grandma had given me a stuffed bear for my birthday, the bear in the picture. I was never without him. That day, we went to the center of town with my dad. Nicolas didn't come with us because he had a stomach bug and stayed in bed. There was a Santa Claus at the main department store. Dad wanted to take me to see him. If I remember correctly, that's because Dad was already hardly ever coming over to see us. So you can imagine how excited I was to go see Santa when he suggested it. I can still feel my hand in my dad's as we walked all the way downtown. In my other hand, I held my stuffed bear, but I wouldn't have let go of my father's hand for anything in the world. We finally got to the front of the line. I won't describe Santa Claus 'cause we all know what he looks like, but I still believed he was real, so seeing him made a big impression on me. When my turn came, he asked me to make a wish and he promised me that he'd make it come true. I hesitated a long time. On one hand, I wanted my bear to talk so the two of us could have real conversations together. On the other hand, I wanted my dad to stay with us forever. I hesitated and hesitated and, in the end, I finally wished for my bear to talk and my dad took the photo of me with Santa.

Except my stuffed bear never said a word. And that was the last time I saw my father. He left and went far away.

For years, I blamed myself. I was sure that if I had asked for my dad to stay with us, he would have stayed. For the longest time, I believed it was my fault that he left. Sometimes, I still wonder. Even if I don't believe in Santa Claus anymore.

Eloise

Lucas holds the letter in his hand for a while. It's not surprising that she didn't want—or, more likely, couldn't bring herself—to read it. His own eyes are stinging.

He hears Eloise's door open. She's just come back.

Without thinking, he bolts upright, heads out into the hallway, and knocks gently on her door.

"Eloise? It's Lucas."

The lock unclicks. Eloise's face appears in the doorway.

"Come in," she whispers.

45

It's dark in the room. Eloise closes the door and pulls Lucas to her. She hugs him tight and the jolt of electricity happens again. Feeling feverish, they press against one another and moan. Eloise puts her lips against the soft skin of his neck. With one movement of his hand, Lucas pushes his sweats to the floor, along with his boxers. Then he pushes on Eloise's shoulders with his palms to lower her to her knees.

"What . . . what are you doing?" she asks, stiffening with surprise.

"Go on, suck me!"

Eloise moves away from him. "Are you nuts? What's gotten into you?"

Lucas does not respond. She senses his hesitation.

"Well, isn't it like that?" he says, finally. "You turn on the lights and you get undressed?"

Eloise chuckles. Lucas knows she's holding back from laughing outright at his pitiful attempt to seem like an experienced guy. With each passing second, it's obvious he is anything but. She comes closer to him in the darkness, rests a hand on his chest, and pulls his sweatshirt over his head, followed by his T-shirt. He hears her getting undressed and slipping into the bed.

"Come here," she calls out to him.

He swiftly removes his sneakers and makes his way over the rug in his socks. The flame of a lighter pierces the dark. Eloise lights a candle on the night table. The meager light dances on the veneer of the headboard.

"Come here," she says again as she gestures toward the empty space beside her.

Lucas lies down, shyly. He brushes his fingers along Eloise's side, searches for her breasts, and starts to caress her. Starts to knead her small breasts.

"Ow, gently!"

"Okay, okay."

He feels Eloise's thin fingers fold around his flaccid penis.

His left hand drifts slowly toward Eloise's belly button as she arches her back and he continues down until he reaches her pubic area. He snatches his hand back as if he just got burned.

He tries to concentrate, to summon "the best of" from all the videos he's watched a thousand times over, but nothing happens. The merest breast on the screen used to give him a hard-on, but here, nothing. Nothing is happening the way it should.

For starters, he thinks Eloise is too thin, too hairy, looks too much like a boy and not enough like the women he fantasized over for such a long time.

Also, he's scared to death of not being up to the deed, so he simply isn't.

Tired of trying, Eloise sits up in bed and turns on the bedside lamp. The weak light reveals a pair of blue leather boxing gloves hanging on a wall. A raggedy stuffed bear that Lucas immediately recognizes sits on the dresser, beneath a poster of a black boxer identified as *Muhammad Ali, 1942–2016.*

Eloise opens her mouth to speak, but Lucas bolts out of bed.

He gathers his stuff in a pile and pulls on his sweatpants.

"Wait, don't leave like that, Lucas, don't be upset," Eloise pleads.

She doesn't have the chance to say anything else. He's already left the room.

She hears him go into his own room, where he slams the door shut in anger.

She reaches her hand out and sighs, grabs her pack of cigarettes she knows are cancer sticks, takes one out, and shouts her own anger to the empty room.

"Piss off!"

46

Lucas gathers momentum, bounces on his heels, and leaps forward. He pierces the blue water of the pool in a perfect dive and attacks the twenty-five-meter length in such a blistering crawl that the lifeguard applauds.

"Way to go! Bravo, Lucas! Keep it up and you'll have a shot at a championship!"

If only the lifeguard knew what was going through Lucas's head at that instant. One—if he could, he'd rush to his computer and connect to a porn site for the rest of the day. He'd immerse himself in the only thing that he has control over in this shitty world: the cyberporn galaxy. Two—arousal guaranteed, relief guaranteed, stress-free, pressure-free, no lousy human interactions to navigate, and, most of all, nothing unexpected. Three—he's seen millions of couplings and could keep a boner for entire days and nights when he watched them on a screen, but he was utterly incapable of one when the right moment came along. Four—what would the shrink have to say about it? She's pretty good. Five—anyway, in this rotten prison, there's no way to access a PC or a smartphone. Six—in fact, ever since what he euphemistically refers to as "the accident," he hasn't gotten an erection. Seven—are all the medications he's taking to blame?

"Go, Delveau! Go!"

Eight—he needs to ask someone, but who is there to ask? Dr. Flohic? Desnoyers?

Nine—

He swims forty laps before he starts to tire out, and then he hoists himself onto the edge of the pool, dripping wet and out of breath. The lifeguard comes over and pokes a finger into Lucas's abdominal muscles.

"Look at that! Damn, the girls are gonna go crazy for you!"

Lucas's face freezes. He turns away and darts off toward the showers.

"What did I say?" the lifeguard shouts after him. "What?"

47

"I don't get it. Is it because of the meds?"

Dr. Desnoyers reviews Lucas's medical file on her computer.

"Possibly, at first," she says. "When you were in the hospital you were put on benzodiazepine. One might say that the treatment rendered you impotent. But the treatment stopped when you started your rehabilitation. Neither the low-dose sleeping pills nor the equally low-dose antidepressants that were prescribed could have prevented you from getting an erection, Lucas. Sorry, but that's not the reason."

The doctor turns away from the computer and looks at him.

"I don't want to know which girl at Poseidon you had this unfortunate encounter with. First, because it's your private life, yours and hers. Second, because even if she spoke to me about it, I wouldn't have the right to tell you. I owe my patients confidentiality."

I'm so ashamed, thinks Lucas. *So ashamed. Of course she*

told the doctor everything. The same sense of humiliation that he's felt a million times since the incident with the selfie floods over him. To put an end to it, he tells Dr. Desnoyers about what happened with Samira.

Dr. Desnoyers listens impassively. She doesn't recoil. He already feels better.

"Same cause, same effect, Lucas. I confess that I actually want to smile. It was clumsy, but, well, you were only fourteen years old, and porn was your only source of reference. Nonetheless, you were lucky that the girl didn't blast the photo all over social media."

Lucas nods.

"This current incident is somewhat similar. But don't worry. Contrary to what you imagine, the problem isn't your impotence, which I think is a temporary condition."

Lucas lifts his head and looks at her, startled.

"So you say. But . . . what am I supposed to do?"

"If I understand what you told me, Lucas, you've been avoiding your friend for the past three days. That's part of the problem. But the way you told me about what happened in the room that day is another."

"But I told you nothing happened," Lucas says, indignant.

"According to you," Dr. Desnoyers objects. "We're going to refer to things properly. You said you immediately asked her to perform fellatio. Which means you had an erection, right?"

Lucas looks at her, defeated. "No. I thought if she did that to me, then I'd get hard."

166

"What is the purpose of an erection, Lucas?"

"Well . . ." He hesitates, like he's taking an oral exam in biology. "To penetrate a woman."

"To penetrate a woman? Can you describe to me the way in which you would like to have a sexual encounter?"

"What? Seriously?"

"I'm not forcing you to answer."

"Okay, well . . . I guess I thought it would be like what I've seen in the porn videos."

"What specifically, Lucas?"

He sighs and looks at the walls around the office as if hoping to find the answers to Dr. Desnoyers's uncomfortable questions.

"Haven't you seen any pornos?"

"That is not the question, Lucas. I want *you* to tell me."

"Well . . ." In one breath he speeds through a list. "BJ, missionary, riding, doggy-style, facial."

Dr. Desnoyers looks at him triumphantly and says, "Thank you, Lucas, that's what I wanted to hear. I needed you to tell me that in order for you to understand what I'm about to explain. I don't judge you, not morally, not physically. I don't judge you as bad because you watched pornos online. It's not necessarily bad to watch porn, even if it is more of an adult entertainment that portrays women in a less-than-ideal way. The problem, your problem, though not limited to you, is that you are addicted to cybersex. We've already spoken about that. Pornography has existed since the time of the Romans. But with the internet, access to porn has changed—there's immediate access to massive amounts of free videos. It's destroyed the lives of women who are underpaid, not to mention that it's illegal."

Lucas jumps. "It's not illegal to watch porn. You have the right to tell me that it's crap, but it's not illegal."

"You're correct, Lucas, it's not illegal to watch porn. What is illegal, however, is to expose minors to pornography. That's for starters. What is also illegal is that millions of videos are pirated. No one cares about that. And it isn't the purpose of my comments. What I'm trying to explain, Lucas, is that the porn you're watching has nothing to do with a genuine sexual relationship you may have with a real person. Porn has entered your head and imagination. You're not the only one who thinks that sex is BJ, missionary, riding, doggy-style, facial. There are plenty of girls who think so too. Girls who think it normal to go from one position to another in a mechanical fashion. Girls who think it normal not to derive any pleasure of their own, who don't listen to themselves and who don't understand why boys want to do all that with them, who do it just because they think that's how it's supposed to be. And it drives them away from boys. Maybe the one you told me about isn't like those girls."

"Maybe she's been with a boy who had erections, at least," Lucas says pitifully.

"Stop fixating on that. The more you think about it, the less it will happen. Let it go. Having an erection isn't always the goal of a relationship."

"Really? What is the goal?"

Dr. Desnoyers explains. "An erection isn't all there is to sex. Nor is it the only way to express desire, and even less, pleasure. You have no obligation to perform. Gentleness, thoughtfulness, listening to one another, yes. But there are all sorts of sexualities. What matters is what you feel when you're with the other person, and even if you feel awkward, it's not so important. The other person might be moved by someone shy and awkward, you know. Tell me, are you in love or merely curious to have sex? If you're simply impatient, then be reassured that it's not a big deal, it's even legitimate. You just turned seventeen."

"In love? How would I know? As for the rest, of course I'm curious."

"Well then, does the girl you talked about interest you as a person?"

"Absolutely," Lucas says without hesitation.

Dr. Desnoyers smiles. "Stop asking yourself questions. Just see what happens."

"That's it?" Lucas asks, thinking that his shrink isn't giving him many answers.

"Yes, for today it is."

Feeling put out, Lucas stands up and zips his sports jacket like he's putting on armor. He stops by the door and turns around.

"Porn is a meat market, Doctor, and it's easy to get served, but it doesn't teach you anything about feelings."

Dr. Desnoyers considers him a moment before responding. "You're making progress, Lucas. You don't realize it, but you are progressing. It's good. Have you found what was missing from your life? What the void you were trying to fill with porn was?"

"I don't know. I'm not sure. I've been asking myself that question these past few days when I've wanted to start up again. Was I trying to fill a void?"

He opens the door.

"You don't necessarily need to steer clear of your friend," Dr. Desnoyers calls out to him. "Time flies by, you know."

48

The *Saint-Quay* is a lobster boat from 1947, with brick-colored sails and a white and sea-blue hull. The old rigging rocks gently in the aluminum-like swell that reflects the zinc color of the sky.

Lucas gets straight to the point. With his ticket in hand, he asks Dr. Flohic's permission to use the telephone.

"You want to call home?"

Lucas shows his voucher for the excursion at sea.

"No, I want to call the office of tourism at Saint-Quay to buy another ticket."

Dr. Flohic's eyes widen. He lets out a whistle. "Well, you're going to have a great time."

"Is it far from here?"

"Hmmm, I'd say it's roughly thirty minutes or so away. You can take the bus. Who are you inviting?"

Lucas does not respond.

"Sorry, I'm being nosy when I shouldn't be," Dr. Flohic says.

He finds the phone number on the internet and hands the receiver to Lucas.

The ticket is less expensive than Lucas expected. He doesn't have a lot of pocket money, but he can afford that price.

His heart pounding in his chest, he goes straightaway to knock on Eloise's door. She opens it, a somber expression coming over her when she sees him. She is about to say something when Lucas sticks the voucher for the boat trip in her hands.

"A good-bye gift!"

"In honor of what?" she grumbles as she reads the wording on the ticket.

Lucas isn't fooled. He sees a glimmer of interest in her eyes.

"Desnoyers reminded me that time flies by. . . ."

"What's she butting in for?"

To appear composed, Lucas stuffs his hands in his pockets.

"Listen, I'm sorry about . . . well, you know. This is a gift, a peace offering. A good-bye present. We can part as friends, good friends, can't we? Otherwise I'll be upset, that much I promise."

Eloise shrugs. "Okay, Lucas."

At the same time, she doesn't invite him inside. She finally gives a weak smile and thanks him, her voice full of sadness.

Before closing the door, she asks, "What about you? Don't you want to go?"

Lucas's face lights up. He tells her that he has a ticket too, and that he bought a second one for her.

"But you can go on your own if you want," he adds.

49

The following morning, Lucas and Eloise takes the bus headed to Saint-Quay.

"What would you have done if I'd refused?"

Eloise asks the question without looking at him, her face turned toward the landscape rushing by outside of the bus window. Lucas doesn't answer right away.

"I wouldn't have gone," he finally says.

This time she's the one who doesn't say anything.

When they get to Saint-Quay and find the sailing vessel, Eloise's face flushes with color. Maybe also because of the wind. She looks at Lucas like a kid on Christmas morning.

"It's beautiful!"

They have to help the instructor hoist the sails, which weigh a ton. That's the way it is on old boats. Lucas thinks about all the sailors who toiled on the rig, generation after generation, and their hard lives. When he turns around, he sees that Eloise is sitting on the roof of the cabin, stuffed into a life jacket, and that she looks a little green. The instructor offers to have her take the helm but she shakes her head no. Half an hour later, she runs to the railing and bends over it to vomit.

Lucas starts to think that his present is quickly turning into a bad idea.

Suddenly the wind picks up. The instructor calls Lucas over and asks him to help hoist a large white sail that immediately billows out in the breeze. It gives the lobster boat an instant kick and it sprints toward the open sea.

• • •

The proud boat heads toward the cliffs of Plouha. Lucas stands by the prow. Eloise joins him, her feet unsteady. She stands beside him. She shivers and lights a cigarette.

"Despite everything, this is really nice."

"Uh-huh," Lucas mumbles as he places a hand on her shoulder.

She snuggles against him, their two life jackets compressed against one another.

"It feels like *Titanic,* doesn't it?" she says. "Although if I hadn't agreed to come, I bet you would've anyway. It just wouldn't be the same."

Lucas laughs. "You're right."

His answer gets lost in the noise of the foam as the bow of the *Saint-Quay* cuts through a larger wave. The wind gains strength and the instructor tells them that they'll have to head back soon.

The half day flies by before they realize it. Lucas is starving. Back at port, he buys a sandwich and offers one to Eloise, who declines.

"Aren't you hungry?"

"I'm still a bit queasy, from the boat," she says. "But I loved it," she adds, placing her hand on Lucas's. "Thank you."

They ride the bus back in silence, the better to prolong the magic of their adventure and to not spoil what brought them together.

When they reach the entrance of the Poseidon, Eloise stops.

"Want to grab a smoke in the garden before we head in?"

Lucas shrugs. "I don't smoke."

"I know, you idiot. But I do."

The wind has died down. It looks as if it's going to rain. They sit on a bench.

"I have to tell you, Eloise. Online games weren't my problem. I was addicted to cybersex. Online porn. I got caught and my parents took all my devices away. I got depressed, and on the day my parents were driving me to see a shrink, I jumped out of the car on the highway. I wanted you to know before you leave."

Eloise doesn't say anything.

"Desnoyers says that I have to find the void I was trying to fill," he adds.

Eloise blows smoke out through her nose. "She tells me that I have to find what I was trying to escape by gaming.

Maybe she's wrong. Maybe I'm the one who was looking to fill a void."

Lucas takes the letter Eloise wrote to him from his pocket and hands it to her.

"I have my take on that," he says. "Maybe I was trying to escape something more than I was trying to fill a void. Who knows?"

Eloise turns to him, their faces very close together, almost touching.

"Good-bye, Lucas," she says. "Thank you."

Her voice is no more than a whisper. She brings her hand around the back of Lucas's neck to bring him still closer, until their mouths come into contact and open. *It's my first kiss,* thinks Lucas. *A soft kiss.* Eloise tastes salty, from the sea spray that blends with the light tobacco. He feels the stud of her tongue piercing roll on his own tongue and the electric jolt happens again. Something else awakens in his belly and spreads to his loins and spine. He presses himself against her and hugs her with all his might. They kiss for maybe one hour, maybe two, he doesn't know, but it's delicious, and when she takes him by the hand and leads him to her room, he follows.

EPILOGUE

LÈVES, SIX MONTHS LATER

Lucas's parents did not come to pick him up. The marriage counselor they were seeing didn't think it was a good idea for Lucas to sit in the back of Marie's car and get on the highway again. On the entire train ride back by himself, Lucas could not stop thinking about Eloise and what had happened between them the afternoon of the boat outing. He thought of their skin touching. Of her scent. Of her breath quickening in his ear. Of the tension he'd felt because he hadn't been in control—hadn't been in control of anything, and had finally accepted it. Of his mounting desire born out of not knowing what Eloise was going to do and do to him. All of it spontaneous. Of their mutual mounting pleasure.

Viewed from the outside, what took place in Eloise's dim room—with Lucas trembling and awkward, and Eloise not very experienced—could pass for a very bad porn film.

Viewed from the inside, what unfolded between them in no way resembled the sad business of staring at a computer screen in solitude—of hours spent with no emotion except for what amounted to sterile arousal.

What Lucas experienced was filled with mystery and wonder. Again and again, they explored and nuzzled each other, and he wished it would never end. He pleaded with her to let him take her back home to Rouen. She refused, but promised to see him again. Soon. To write to him. Soon.

Sebastian and Marie waited for him in front of the train station at Chartres. They stood side by side but seemed like two strangers, and if this wasn't what they had become, Lucas soon realized that they were irreparably estranged.

His suspicions were confirmed when they got back to the house and his parents announced that they had decided to separate. After the accident, they had started couples ther-apy and had reached the conclusion that they had fallen out of love. Sebastian found an apartment not far from the ten-nis club. He had been living there for two months already. He had left the house to Marie. They explained that their feelings for him would never change. Lucas wasn't terribly saddened by the news, nor was he surprised. He listened to his parents as he stroked Cuddles, the cat's eyes becoming slits, his tail whipping the air as he purred happily in Lucas's arms.

Lucas did not want to return to high school. He quickly found a part-time job at the local McDonald's. He started correspondence classes to get his diploma. He sent his homework for review over the internet. His reunion with the computer was detached. Out of caution, he limited his daily time spent in front of the screen. Instead, he swam a lot, training hard, with an eye toward the regional championships and competing in the four-hundred-meter breaststroke, a challenge where his slight limp isn't a handicap.

In spite of the promises they exchanged, Lucas never saw Eloise again. For a time they stayed in touch by email. She was doing well. She had celebrated her eighteenth birthday at her grandmother's. She had found a short-term full-time job at a computer store in Rouen and had moved into an apartment with a friend. On multiple occasions, they had sworn to get together. They had even fixed a date. Lucas was supposed to join Eloise in Rouen, but at the last minute she had canceled. In her message, she said he wasn't to blame, that what had happened between them was amazing, but that she had trouble seeing him again, the same way she had trouble with everything from that time in her life. A time, she added, from which she wanted to break entirely. Lucas persisted. Soon after, she stopped answering his emails. It's hard to forget your first time. Even if he wanted to, he knows that he could never erase Eloise from his memory.

Even though he tells himself that Eloise may not be wrong.

Although he still feels the need to talk regularly to a psychologist, Lucas has never gone back on a porn site. He no longer has the interest. Lately Emma, a small, muscular blonde on the girls' Eure-and-Loir swim team, has captured his attention. He even worked up the courage to talk to her last week.

From time to time, he still thinks about Dr. Clara Desnoyers and the question she asked him. If he met her now, he knows what his answer would be.

It's no longer time to flee. It's time to live.

AUTHOR'S NOTE

The ease and frequency with which we connect to online social networks has never been greater. Young or old, we're all guilty of connecting way more than we should. Children and teenagers are especially susceptible to confusing the virtual world for the real one. All too quickly, they can start feeling more alive and more at home in a virtual landscape. That's when addictions take root.

While I was researching online recruitment by terrorist groups for my previous YA novel, I had occasion to talk to students and teachers about the dependence adolescents have on their screens, and on online games and cybersex. The latter, in particular, grabbed my attention, probably because the moral aspect of cybersex makes it a subject less frequently addressed than, say, gaming. Tackling the topic of cybersex involves risks—it's an inherently dark and sleazy world. But the suffering that stems from cybersex addiction is no less valid than the suffering from any other compulsive habit. It simply receives less coverage; it goes largely unreported.

As I began to read studies of children who view online porn, I was shocked by the statistics: 66 million to 110 million young people connect to porn sites yearly, worldwide. And the numbers are increasing each year.

Typically, first exposure to online porn happens when children are as young as eight to eleven years old. The exposure is often involuntary—a random click—with 5 percent of these kids eventually becoming addicted. It's a dependency that can damage the sexuality of a child and lead to lifelong habits where the only "intimate" contact with another human being happens in front of a screen.

My research was exhaustive. Not only did I talk to teenagers and teachers about various online addictions, but I also spent time with young people in a post-rehab center and with the center's staff psychologist. I spoke to David Le Breton, eminent professor at the University of Strasbourg, who is both an anthropologist and a sociologist, as well as an expert in the high-risk behavior of adolescents. I went to Marmottan Hospital in Paris, which since 2015 has had a program dedicated to treating cybersex addictions. There I met with a psychiatrist focused on sex therapy. The hospital librarian sent me numerous articles. I read countless books on pornography. I also watched lots of porn videos, on numerous sites, covering different categories of porn. I watched documentaries, read dissertations, and more.

As a writer, I like exploring the shades of gray that make us human. I'm convinced that our consumer society operates exactly like the porn industry: desire alternates with frustration to beget a new desire that, once satisfied, begets a new frustration, and so on.

Lucas is the hero of *Point of View*. On the outside, he seems like an average teenage geek. At least that's what his parents believe him to be. But once his addiction to online porn is revealed, his virtual world crumbles, and so does he. He has a long, hard journey to being a whole person again.

As I wrote this book, I did not want to make judgments. I have not judged Lucas. I have not judged his parents. I have not judged any of the characters. I merely want readers to have empathy for Lucas and be aware that help and recovery are possible.

Patrick Bard

If you want more information about addiction, or to get help for yourself or someone you know, you can contact mental health organizations and hotlines online. The following resource is a good place to start:

Substance Abuse and Mental Health Administration
www.samhsa.gov/find-help/national-helpline
1-800-662-HELP (4357)

ABOUT THE AUTHOR

Patrick Bard is a novelist, travel writer, and photojournalist. His many novels for adults and young adults have received prestigious awards in his native France. *Point of View* is his first novel to be translated into English.

ABOUT THE TRANSLATOR

Françoise Bui spent twenty years as an executive editor at Delacorte Press, an imprint of Random House Children's Books, where her list of edited books included numerous novels in translation. Of these, four received the American Library Association's Mildred L. Batchelder Award, and two were Honor titles. Originally from France, Françoise lives in New York City.